The Promise Paperback Copyright © 2021 Lorhainne Ekelund
Editor: Talia Leduc

ISBN-13: 978-1990590450

Give feedback on the book at:
lorhainneeckhart.le@gmail.com

Twitter: @LEckhart
Facebook: AuthorLorhainneEckhart

Printed in the U.S.A

THE PROMISE

The Friessens (Jed & Diana)

LORHAINNE ECKHART

The Outsider Series

The Forgotten Child (Brad and Emily)
A Baby and a Wedding
Fallen Hero (Andy, Jed, and Diana)
The Search
The Awakening (Andy and Laura)
Secrets (Jed and Diana)
Runaway (Andy and Laura)
Overdue
The Unexpected Storm (Neil and Candy)
The Wedding (Neil and Candy)

The Friessens: A New Beginning

The Deadline (Andy and Laura)
The Price to Love (Neil and Candy)
A Different Kind of Love (Brad and Emily)
A Vow of Love, A Friessen Family Christmas

The Friessens

The Reunion
The Bloodline (Andy & Laura)
The Promise (Diana & Jed)
The Business Plan (Neil & Candy)

The Decision (Brad & Emily)
First Love (Katy)
Family First
Leave the Light On
In the Moment
In the Family: A Friessen Family Christmas
In the Silence
In the Stars
In the Charm
Unexpected Consequences
It Was Always You
The First Time I Saw You
Welcome to My Arms
Welcome to Boston
I'll Always Love You
Ground Rules
A Reason to Breathe
You Are My Everything
Anything For You
The Homecoming includes FREE short story When
They Were Young
Stay Away From My Daughter
The Bad Boy
A Place to Call Our Own
The Visitor
All About Devon
Long Past Dawn
How to Heal a Heart
Keep Me In Your Heart

The Friessens Family

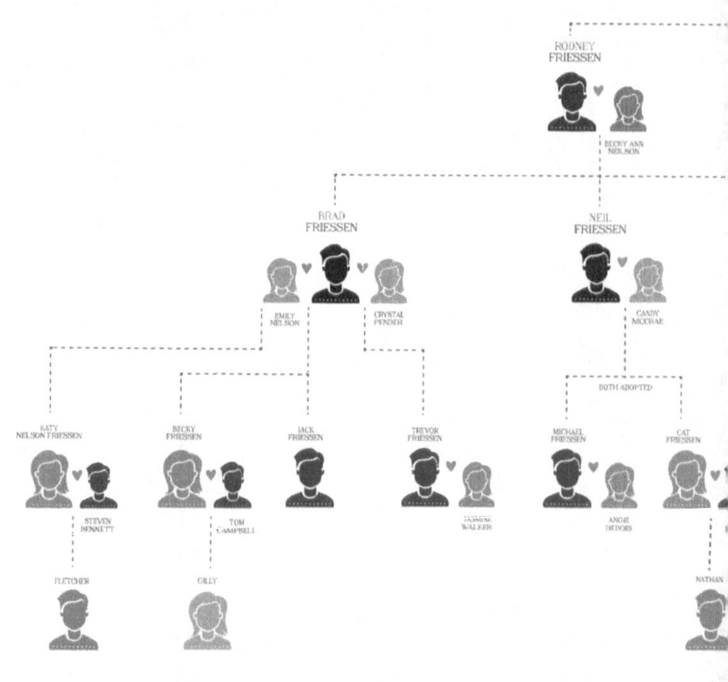

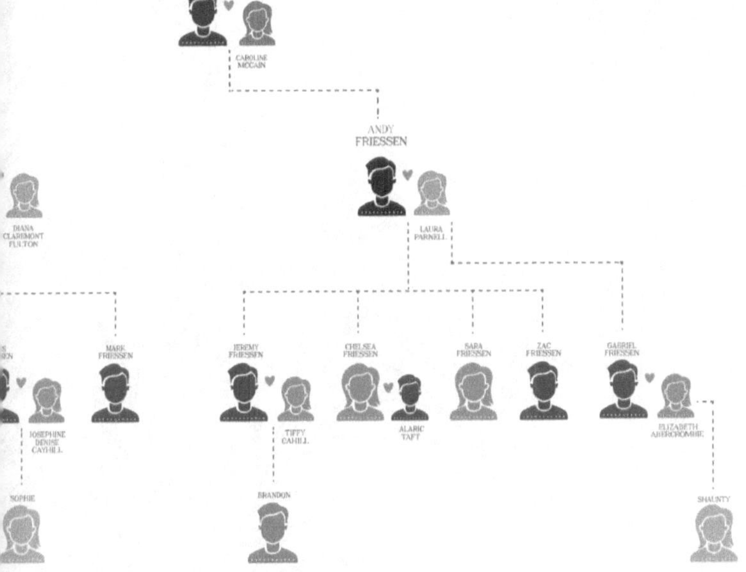

The Friessens

NTIRE FRIESSEN FAMILY	LEAVE THE LIGHT ON	KATY & STEVEN
& LAURA	IN THE MOMENT	BECKY & TOM *introducing you to a new character Vic McCabe which then launches a new series, The McCabe Brothers*
DIANA	IN THE FAMILY. *A Friessen Family Christmas*	THE ENTIRE FRIESSEN FAMILY
& CANDY	IN THE SILENCE	CAT & XANDER
& EMILY	IN THE STARS	DANNY & EVIE
& STEVEN	IN THE CHARM	CHRIS & J.D.
& STEVEN	UNEXPECTED CONSEQUENCES	CHRIS & J.D. *and Danny & Evie*

The Friessens

IT WAS ALWAYS YOU	KATY & STEVEN
THE FIRST TIME I SAW YOU	GABRIEL & ELIZABETH
WELCOME TO MY ARMS	CHELSEA & ALARIC
WELCOME TO BOSTON	PAIGE & MORGAN *A Friessen Family short story*
I'LL ALWAYS LOVE YOU	JEREMY
GROUND RULES	JEREMY & TIFFY
A REASON TO BREATHE	TREVOR
YOU ARE MY EVERYTHING	MICHAEL

"Lorhainne Eckhart is one of my go to authors when I want a guaranteed good book. So much love and such a strong sense of family."

Lori W.

"Tissue's. You deserve an award for the best written books I have read in a long time."

Sonya

"The one thing that I always love about this series is that it shows that at times it does take a village. That we all are all human and make mistakes, and that with family and those that we love our mistakes are redeemable. I cannot wait to read what's next."

Amber T.

Falling in love with Jed Friessen was a dream come true.

Married to Jed, Diana has a family and is living her happily ever after. She knew heartbreak and suffering as a child, and the pain of rejection, but she now understands what it means to be loved.

However, when the past comes knocking on her door, reminding her of everything she's left behind, everything she was, and everything she's lost, her guilt and doubt threaten the life she's built with her husband.

Chapter 1

There were two realities. The first was her picture-perfect life in the countryside on a ranch with her handsome and overly protective husband, Jed, and their two little boys, Danny, five, and Christopher, three. It was her happily ever after, and nothing bad could ever touch her there. In the second, Diana Friessen, daughter of the town whore, would forever be tainted by the sins of her mother, always having to remind herself she was worthy of being loved.

It was difficult, if not downright impossible some days, to process her past, which she had long since separated from the person she was now. Who was Diana Friessen? She had defined herself for so long by surviving, by carrying the weight of someone else's wrongs. She had brought that weight into her picture, making the ache, the pain, and the hurt part of her story until she left, only to return years later and be swept off her feet by love.

She was loved by Jed. She could see how much she was a part of him from the moments they spent together and everything he did for her. He wanted—no, needed to have her here at home, raising his boys. She had once believed this was because he didn't want to compete with her career, and truth be told, Jed was not a man who could ever come second. He wasn't made that way, and she didn't think she could love a man who could settle for the bits and pieces tossed his way. He was her everything, and she'd given up all she'd chosen just to be his. He had built a business conducting horse clinics, working with children, some with special needs. He was an amazing man, and he filled her with such hope and completeness that she would never have loneliness as her bed partner again.

She'd give it all up again, too, even though she loved knowing she had a law degree, an achievement all her own, and she could begin a practice at any time. It was something she'd begun thinking of more and more as of late: having something that was just hers.

"What are you thinking?" Jed slid his hand around her stomach, pulling her against him so she could feel all his hardness and the way his amazing body molded against hers. They were made for each other, and she loved how she fit him so perfectly, comfortably. He pressed his cheek, which was rough with whiskers from two days without shaving, against hers.

She reached her hand back to touch him, his face, his head, as he held her as he always did, in a way that let her know he'd never let her fall.

"Oh, life and things," she said as he kissed her cheek, and of course she smiled, as being loved by Jed was something she had to remind herself every day never to take for granted. He gave her all of himself.

"Tell me," he said without letting her go as she swayed against him.

"I was thinking of a lot of things, how you make me feel safe, and for so long I've felt as if I could finally heal, knowing you were taking care of everything, me and the kids, and just being loved by you." She sighed, and he didn't say anything but slid his other arm around her front, over her breasts, and then held her shoulder, wrapping her up in him so she could touch his wrist and hold on. "I realized, too, I'm not who I used to be."

"Sounds like you're bothered by something." He kissed her cheek again as she breathed deeply, relaxing.

"Not so much bothered but considering." She noticed a car coming down their long driveway in the distance. With the dust and the fact that they lived so far out of town on flat land she could see for miles, no one could sneak up on them. "You expecting anyone?" She started to straighten when Jed stepped to her side, sliding his hand around her hip, holding her to him.

"No," he replied.

She didn't say anything else, her stomach knotting at the sight of a faded blue compact.

For a minute, she wished Jed would say something, because he had to know how uncomfortable she was. The man could read her like no other, and she couldn't hide anything from him.

"Isn't that…?" He stopped, frowning, as the car pulled up in front of the small house, zipping in beside Diana's SUV.

Diana's hand slid up to her throat on instinct. She wasn't sure whether she had gasped until Jed touched her arm, drawing her gaze to him. She hadn't realized he'd been watching her.

"I can't believe this. Your mother is back. What the hell is she thinking, after I sent her on her way?" Jed sounded really mad, and Diana didn't have a chance to answer when the car door shut.

"Oh, hi there!" Faye Claremont said as she darted around the front of the car in a light blue T-shirt and matching pencil skirt, wearing inch-high sandals. Her deep red hair was brushed back into a ponytail, her lips painted bright red, and she had a curvy body that screamed sex. "Well, just looky here at all you've done to this place. It's looking mighty fine from when I was here last." She stopped at the bottom of the stairs, taking in the one-story house and the addition Jed had built. It had white siding, green trim, and a front deck with a finished railing. Diana wanted to scream at her to shut up.

Jed said nothing as he glanced between Diana and her mother. "And when exactly was that?" he asked. For a moment, Faye's bright vivid smile faltered before she stepped on the bottom of the stairs.

"Why, just last week. Didn't Diana tell you I stopped by?"

She could feel Jed's fingers digging in to her hips, holding her to him as she touched the railing of the front deck, which looked over the acres of flat land. She looked away to the barn and indoor arena where Jed held his clinics. She could hear a horse nicker from the barn, and she swallowed, her tongue thick, unsure of what the hell to say, wishing she could crawl away and hide. Yes, her mother had stopped by not once but twice after how many years? It had rocked Diana's world, and each time had been unannounced. Faye was trying to worm her way back into her life, or so it seemed.

"So what can I do for you, Faye?" Jed said, not giving a hint that somehow, he and Diana could keep secrets from each other.

"Well, I wanted to see my daughter and try to make amends, and I feel as if we're making some real progress. Ain't that right, baby?" Faye smiled brightly to Diana, and she wondered whether Jed could hear the strangled noise she was making or if it was all in her head.

"Faye, I made it very clear to you the first time that you're not to come back here. I don't want you coming around here, upsetting my wife." Jed was quite direct, and Diana also knew he'd likely have a word or two with her later. The overwhelming guilt ate away at her, because she hadn't shared with Jed the fact that Faye Claremont had ignored his decree and kept coming back. Even now, she couldn't explain why.

"That isn't my intention. It was never my intent to cause any upset to my daughter, and I feel honestly that we were making progress." She was looking toward Diana, and this time Jed was also staring down at her.

"Why do you keep coming here? I didn't ask you to come." Diana had finally found her voice, and it sounded so strange, so weak.

"I need to make amends, and I told you that. I can't even begin to make things right after what happened, being taken from you. I just had a lot of years to think about it, and you're my daughter. No matter what's happened, I know there's no excuse for what I put you through. I made a lot of bad choices. I know that now."

"Faye." Jed leaned on the railing, resting on his forearms, looking down on her. He was no longer touching Diana, but he hadn't moved from her side. "I appreciate you wanting to make amends to my wife, but I was also clear that you weren't to come back here and were to leave my wife be. I don't take kindly to anyone messing with my wife, hurting her, upsetting her. You understand that your bridge here has already burned." He said it so calmly and flicked his hand toward her, but there was no mistaking his meaning.

Faye flashed her big blue eyes, smiling up at him. What was she thinking, trying to turn the charm on Diana's husband? Maybe she realized her mistake, as she suddenly dialed it back a bit. This was the first time she'd had a chance to admire Jed, to ogle him, but she must have understood clearly that Jed was not the man for her to be setting her sights on. Diana wanted to smack her for crossing that line.

"You're a very lucky woman, Diana, to have a husband like the one you have. I'd have given anything for it, but it wasn't in the cards for me. I did the best I could, and maybe that wasn't good enough. It was what it was." She opened her purse and pulled out a pamphlet, then stepped closer and held it out, but Jed reached around Diana and took it. She couldn't make herself look at it, just stared at the woman who'd given birth to her, whom Diana favored, who'd made her childhood hell and made her doubt everything good in her life.

"It's my group." Faye gestured to the paper Jed was holding. "We meet on Thursdays, and I'd really like you to come." Instead of pushing, going on and on as she always had about everything, her life and her crap, she stepped back, looking sadly over at Diana before turning and walking back to her car, where she slid behind the wheel.

As Faye drove away, leaving a trail of dust behind her, Jed turned to Diana and said, "So how about you explain why you lied to me?"

Chapter 2

Seeing the haunted look on his wife's face made Jed want to hold her even as he fought the urge to shake her and yell at her. What the hell had she been thinking, allowing her mother back here and then keeping it from him?

He did none of that, though. Instead, he crossed his arms, and Diana just stood there as if trying to figure out what to say. Her deep red vibrant hair was now touching her shoulders. She had chopped her long waves into a boyish shag after her mother had shown up all those months ago, because she feared being anything like her mother. He'd thought Faye had only been there one time, especially after he'd warned her not to come back. What had Diana been thinking?

"I didn't lie to you, Jed. I wouldn't do that. I didn't tell you she came, is all."

"That's the same in my book, and you know it, Diana. It's lying by omission. Hasn't this already been played out in our lives?" He kept his hands right where they were even though he was tempted to put them on her shoulders. That would be a mistake, with the way he was feeling. "It makes me wonder if there isn't more you're keeping from me."

She flinched as if he'd slapped her. "No. I'm not hiding things from you. You make me sound so awful." The emotion in her voice, the way she said it, should have been enough to convince him.

"Well, what am I to think when I find out Faye's been here again and you've said nothing? Did you invite her?"

Her eyes widened. "You must think pretty low of me, Jed, to believe I would invite my mother here. I didn't want her to come back. She just showed up, and you weren't here." She stepped away, running her fingers through her hair and then pressing her palm to her fore-head, shutting her eyes. She opened her mouth to say something, but nothing more than a squeak came out.

"What, Diana? Talk to me. What's going through that head of yours?" He just watched her, waiting out this internal struggle she couldn't hide from him.

"She was here twice. She keeps saying she wants to make up for what happened."

"And?" He gestured toward her.

"She's Faye, and I can't shake this little voice that pops up in my head telling me she's still my mother. I know it's sick and twisted that I think I owe her some-thing, but I hear her say to me over and over that she's my mother and she wants a second chance. She wants me to forgive her. She'd like a do-over. I know, Jed, from the way you're looking at me, that there's no way she should be setting one foot here, and I should send her away, but part of me feels abandoned and wants to be able to forgive her. Then I'm disgusted with myself for thinking it. That's why I didn't say anything, because I don't want you looking at me the way you are now." Her hand was shaking as she held it up, gesturing.

"Diana, the way I'm looking at you now is because you should have told me you were thinking this way, feeling this way. Yeah, I would have told you to stop it and then gone on to convince you how wonderful and kind and good you are until you believe it—because you are. You have a family now, and Faye may have given birth to you, but she isn't your mother. I don't understand why you have this need to forgive her, but I'm not going to tell you not to. All I can say is she'll never have my forgiveness, and I don't want her messing with you again. You keeping it a secret isn't okay, Diana. We made a lot of promises to each other, and when I put my ring on your finger and made you my wife, I promised to love and protect you. We said a lot of other things to each other, too, but that you would be keeping things from me wasn't one of them. I'll have your promise now, Diana. No more secrets. No more not telling me your mother's showing up here and pressuring you to make things right."

She rested her hands on his arms, and he stepped closer to her, running his hands over her shoulders and her pale shirtsleeves. She was looking up at him. "That goes both ways, though, Jed. We share everything. That means you, too."

Damn woman. There were things he couldn't and wouldn't share with her, so he looked away. More than anything, it was his job, his role, to look after her.

"Jed? I mean it. You want my promise, then I'll have yours."

He sighed and was trying to figure out how she could turn things as she was. "I'm your husband. I promised to protect you, and I'll do that however I need to. It's not the same."

Diana allowed her hand to fall away as she stepped back and stared out into the sun. "You know what, Jed? I love you very much, but you can be so hypocritical. It doesn't work that way, where you expect everything from me, my thoughts, my feelings, for me to share everything, but not the same of yourself. Do you not remember before when you did this, falling from the barn roof, almost dying, leaving me to find out how dire our finances were?"

"Diana," he started, but he had to stop as he thought of all he'd never shared with his wife. That had been one time. He'd tried to protect her and hold everything together. After all, it was his job to look after his family. "Everything I never shared was to protect you. You know that," he said—but there was also the secret of his mother and the affair she'd had with his uncle. Just learning the ugly truth a few weeks before had been hard on Jed and his brothers, Brad and Neil. It had been hard on his cousin, Andy, too. It had rocked all of them and was his parents' secret, something he couldn't divulge. "Some things aren't mine to share," he said.

"I see." Diana was pulling away from him, and she glanced at her watch. "I need to go pick up Danny and Cristopher from school." She didn't look at him as she walked into the house and came back out a few minutes later with her purse and keys, and she didn't glance his way as she went down the steps. She was halfway to her SUV when he called out to her.

"Diana!"

She stopped, and he didn't miss how she stiffened. She didn't turn around, but after a second, she did turn her head, fighting not to look his way.

"We've been through a lot of things, Diana, but you walking away mad like this is you being unreasonable." Jed didn't like this wall between them, and walking away from one another wasn't something they did.

"Well, Jed, the problem is you seem to think it's a one-way street. I share everything with you, give everything to you, and walk away from all I've had for you, but you give up nothing of yourself, share what you choose, and hide from me what you think I can't handle. It's really sad that you think so little of me."

This time she climbed in her SUV and drove away.

For the first time, Jed suspected that his comfortable life, and his right to have everything he'd ever wanted as he wanted it, suddenly wasn't so perfect after all.

Chapter 3

She listened to Jed reading Christopher and Danny one of their favorite bedtime stories about a donkey and an owl. It was one she'd heard a hundred times, so many that she remembered the words. She listened to her little boys and the excitement in their voices, and of course she could picture the animation on Jed's face as he read, his children curled up against him, one on each side, held by a father who loved them. His love, out of everything, could never be questioned.

He did love them, deeply. He was there for his children, raising them, always there to lend a hand to Diana. He was such a good father, lover, and best friend. She squeezed the sponge and dumped it into the sink. She wouldn't trade him for anything, even though he made her so angry at times that she wanted to scream. She also knew, if she allowed herself to admit it, that keeping things from her was Jed's way of protecting her, but she wanted a little more now. She wanted him to know she wasn't some fragile, broken thing who couldn't handle hearing something bad. She was stronger than that. She knew he needed to keep her safe, but why did he have to see her as so weak?

"Can we talk?"

She jumped, her heart skipping a beat. She hadn't heard her husband come in, and there he was, standing just outside the kitchen, watching her. Asking to talk wasn't something he did. In fact, any time she asked that same question, she'd see something in his eyes as if he wanted to head for the hills.

She nodded, feeling the anger she'd felt this afternoon kick up again. As she stepped forward, she crossed her arms so she wouldn't be tempted to touch him. This time, she had to hold her ground and stand firm. It was so easy for Jed to get her to see things his way.

"Diana, why are you so mad? What is this really about?"

Was he kidding? "You're treating me as if I'll break."

He was shaking his head. "You don't get it, do you?" He wasn't giving an inch. In fact, he stepped closer to her so he was in her space, and she had to look up into his handsome face. He still hadn't shaved, and his brown hair was a little mussed, probably from running his fingers through it and from the cowboy hat he wore all day every day when he was outside. His scent always comforted her. She wanted to lean in. Her body craved him.

"Enlighten me, Jed, because I'm feeling as if everything in this marriage is one sided."

"This isn't about that." He stepped in closer, his body touching her. "This is about me being so in love with you and remembering all the pain and hurt you carried when we met for what you survived as a child, what you had lived through with your mother. You were like this wounded spirit who's now healing, and when she showed up here that first time, I've never seen a fear like that in you. When you didn't tell me she came back…" He jabbed his hand toward the door. "That woman has an agenda, and you kept it from me when she had the nerve to show up here again. I'm your husband. Someone messes with you, they mess with me, and when you don't tell me Faye's been here, it says you don't trust me, or you're hiding something, and we don't hide things from each other, not like this."

He was right about that, but she also wondered what it was he was keeping from her, because Jed kept secrets, and now she knew there was something else he was hiding.

"All right, I agree, but I didn't keep it from you because I don't trust you. I don't know why I didn't say anything, other than I was trying to sort it through in my own mind. She's my mother. It's my past, which I have to come to peace with, and it's my fear that what she did will somehow touch you and the boys like it did me. Then days passed, and I couldn't say anything."

"But that's what I'm saying, Diana. It's not all on you. I need you to tell me, not hide things from me."

She raised her hands and fisted them when she wanted to take hold of his shirt and touch him.

"Husband and wife, Diana. No secrets," he said again.

"Okay, I get it, no secrets. That means you, too, Jed. Whatever it is that you're hiding, that you're holding on to, it's not fair of you to think you have the right to hide a part of yourself from me. You just said it: We're husband and wife." She gestured to her ring finger, to his ring, and this time he placed his large hand over hers, holding it against his chest.

"I'm not hiding anything of myself or a part of me from you, Diana."

She could tell there was something he wasn't saying. "Yes, but you do keep things from me—even what you said to my mother the first time you sent her away. You had me go into the house, and yes, I was grateful when you took care of it, but you never told me what you said."

He just watched her, his gaze heavy. "I told her that if she messed with you, it would be the same as messing with me, and I wouldn't allow it. I told her she wasn't to set foot back here again, because she wouldn't like my reaction. Apparently, she didn't listen to my friendly warning." He lifted his hand to touch her face, sliding the back of his fingers over her cheek.

She gripped his hand. "Okay," she said, nodding. He had told her, but she also knew there was something else, and it was a puzzle she would have to figure out. "There's more, though, something else you don't want to tell me about. If it's not about you, it's someone else."

By the way he pulled away from her, she could tell she was close to something.

"Your family?" she said. "Something happened?"

This time, he did turn away, rubbing his hand up the back of his head. When he turned to her, she knew she'd nailed it. It was in his expression. "Diana, it's not my secret to share, or I'd tell you. And before you compare this to you hiding your mother showing up here—well, don't, because it isn't about me or something that affects us in any way. It doesn't."

She could tell he was quite bothered by whatever it was. "Jed, is it something that happened in your family, with your brothers…with Andy?"

He gave her an exasperated look, shaking his head.

"No, it's not them, but they know. Look, Diana, don't keep poking down this road. It's something I was never meant to know. It's not my secret to share. I promised I wouldn't."

Well, this was a puzzle. If it wasn't Neil or Brad or Andy, who was it? "Not your parents?" she said, seeing a hurt on Jed's face that she'd never seen before. Something was bothering him. She was getting warmer, and this game was not something her husband was taking kindly to.

"Look. Drop it, please, because I don't want this in my head. I love my mom and dad, they're the best parents ever, and they were there for us growing up. They were our rock, and learning something about their past that doesn't put them in a good light…I don't want to know it. Would you want Danny and Christopher to know about everything your mom did, what you lived through?"

Whatever happened, she could see how much it bothered him. "No, I wouldn't, but if the time came that I had to tell them, I would."

This time, Jed was shaking his head. "Well, Diana, this…" He gestured to his head and took a breath as if he couldn't finish. "I don't want you to know because it puts my mom in a bad light, and I've had a hard time, the last few days they were here, tiptoeing around and making sure she didn't know I'd found out. I promised Dad. We all did, after finding out something this bad. So let it go, please. I don't want you seeing Mom for anything other than who she is now."

Now she was scared, and she ached for her husband and his mother, whom she loved dearly. "Jed, do you have any idea what you're saying? When you leave me hanging like that, I'm starting to think some pretty bad things, probably way worse than what happened…"

"She had an affair with Uncle Todd!" he shouted, then stepped back as if he couldn't believe what he'd said.

Whoa! It took a second for her to realize how horrible this was for him. "No, Jed, not your mom. That's my mother, not yours."

"You just couldn't stop pushing," he said. "I'm sorry, I shouldn't have told you. It's something you shouldn't have in your head, and I sure as hell shouldn't, either."

As she stood there, trying to figure out what to say, Jed turned, reached for his hat, and opened the front door.

"I'm going to feed the horses," he said, and the door closed.

Diana watched her husband from the window as he walked toward the barn. She wished she'd listened to Jed and not pushed so hard, because his mother's deep dark secret was something she didn't feel entitled to know. "Oh, Jed, I'm so sorry," she whispered.

Chapter 4

He couldn't believe he'd told his wife when he was doing everything he could to try to forget what he'd learned. She had kept pushing, though he admitted to himself that she was partly right. He had expected to know everything about what she was doing, thinking, and feeling, yet he hadn't done the same. He had tried to justify his behavior by telling himself he was protecting her, and to a point he had been.

"Hey," Diana said, perching on the bed behind him, putting her hands on his shoulders and squeezing the tenseness. She smelled of lavender from the bath she'd been in moments before. He could have joined her, but he'd been sitting on the end of the bed, just trying to figure out some things. "You okay?" She kissed his shoulder, rubbing her hands over the cotton of his worn red shirt.

"Hmm," he grunted, not really wanting to talk anymore but enjoying very much where her hands were lingering.

"I'm sorry, Jed. I don't know what to say about your mom. Did she really have an affair with Todd? I don't understand how or why. Your mom is so…"

He turned around and faced Diana, taking in the confusion in her expression and the mixed emotions he knew his dad didn't want any of them displaying around Becky. "She still is, Diana. She's not your mother."

He stood up and moved away from her, pulling his shirt over his head, and she was still sitting there on the bed, wrapped in a pink satin robe, her hair wet on the edges and pinned up. She was beautiful, and he didn't like her thinking badly of his mom.

"Don't misunderstand me, Jed. I would never compare Becky to my mother. They're not the same. Your mom has been there for all of us, for me, for you. She loves us, and I just don't understand how this could have happened. Was it recent?"

She placed her hand softly on the bed as if willing him to tell her everything. It pissed him off to have to relive it and talk it to death, considering the thought of it turned his stomach.

"No, it wasn't. It was before me, and it was something we were never meant to know about. Leave it to good old Uncle Todd to hurt everyone. He said enough about Mom that Dad and him got into it. Brad, Neil, and I were there with Andy. It was bad, but he told us what happened and made us promise not to share it, not even with you. Dad and Mom buried that part of their life. It was awful hearing about it, but they were young and had both made mistakes. They put it behind them. Do you really need to know the gory details? I don't want to have that picture in my head anymore. I'm doing my damnedest to get it out!" He hadn't realized he was shouting until he took in the sympathy pouring from Diana.

She shook her head. "No, you're right, I don't. I'm sorry, Jed, because your mom is a good person. She's the kind of mother I always wished I had. I can't imagine how you're feeling."

"How I'm feeling is that I'd like to get some sleep before the boys descend on us in the morning. I've got to get the horses ready, as a new clinic is starting soon."

The number of special needs kids Jed was working with had continued to grow, now including a varying range of disabilities. Turning away kids was not something he'd ever imagined they would have to do, but helping them all just wasn't realistic. He had staff who came and walked the kids on horseback, taught them how to work, groom, and just be with a horse. It was a nice business, something that was close to Diana's heart, as well.

"Do you need help tomorrow?" she said.

He just shook his head. "Not much for you to do. Once the staff get here, they have it handled."

Maybe it was the way she watched him that made him realize that swaddling her like he was, leaving her here with just the kids, was not helping. "But come and give me a hand after you take the boys in to school."

Her face lit up, and she pushed off the bed toward him. "Yeah, that would be fun."

It would be nice to have her with him, since she was more often running after the boys, and having all this time to think wasn't doing her any good. He leaned in and kissed her as she ran her hands over his chest and around his back.

"So no more secrets?" He slid his hands over her face

as he watched the light fill her deep blue eyes, and she became so solemn for a moment that his stomach tightened as if she were about to drop another bomb. He didn't think he could take much more today.

"I've been thinking about a few things. Not sure how you'll feel about them, though," she said, sounding awfully mysterious.

"And?" He allowed his hands to fall, skimming down her sides, holding her to him.

"Having Andy and Laura here was wonderful, but it also stirred some things inside me."

He'd wondered when she was going to talk to him. He'd seen the way she'd fawned all over Sarah, Andy and Laura's new baby girl. He'd seen the longing, and truth be told, he wanted more children, to build this family to something truly spectacular. "You want another baby," he said. "I saw the way you looked at Sarah. A girl would be nice, although there're no guarantees. We can just keep trying, though."

She touched his face, but she wasn't smiling. "The idea of having a daughter is something I've thought of, and it would be nice."

His heart sank. The way she was saying it had him realizing that maybe Diana wasn't interested in any more kids, and that thought made him sad. "You don't want any more?"

"It's not that, Jed. I love being a mother, but having to pour over Andy's mother's will, being a lawyer again even for a short time, it was a part of my brain that I feel I've let go. I felt needed in a way that made me feel important."

This was not what he wanted to hear, and he stepped back, taking a look at Diana, trying to figure out what had come over her.

"Jed, don't do that. Don't look at me as if I've betrayed you. I love being a mother, your wife, being here."

"It sounds to me like you're talking about taking up practicing law, and here I thought you wanted another baby. Now it sounds as if that's not good enough." Saying it out loud made him sound like a jerk, he realized, but he couldn't rein in that part of him that wanted to control everything about Diana's world.

"I want a houseful with you and wouldn't give any of this up."

"I don't understand why you're talking about being a lawyer, then, because that would be a lot of time away from the boys, away from us. I've got the programs we're running here for the kids, and the trail rides still. I have my hands full here, and I need you to be able to do all this."

She went to him and touched his arms, his face, trying to calm him, but the thought of his wife giving her attention to something else was making him crazed.

"Jed, whoa, you're jumping so far ahead to Z when I'm still at A. I do not want to take my attention from you or the boys, do you hear me? I'm still their mom, I'm still your wife, but there is a lot more to me than that, and there's time now with the boys starting kindergarten and Christopher in preschool three days a week. I could do some small stuff from home. Just a few hours here and there is all I'm talking about. I'm not looking to set up shop in town and be away from my kids all day, from you. There's more to me than doing laundry and washing dishes, Jed."

He didn't like it, because although a few hours a week was fine, he knew the kind of problems that crept up and would land on Diana's doorstep. In the end, they would end up taking all her attention.

"I don't like it, Diana, because even though you say it will only be a few hours, I know the kind of person you are. That's one of the reasons I love you so much. Your heart is so big and full that you couldn't walk away. You give everything to whatever it is you're doing, and thankfully that's been here." He gestured to the house around them.

"Jed, how can you say that? I wouldn't put you and the boys second."

"Diana, stop it. I know you better than you know yourself. You think it's going to be small and easy and manageable, but something will always come out of the woodwork, and no matter how you plan it, you won't be able to turn your back on that person." He took in her wide eyes and exasperation. She was trying to convince him and couldn't figure out how. He reached for her chin and brushed his thumb over her soft pink lips. "Your heart is so big, you want to help everybody, but you're only you. I love you for your vulnerability and that big heart of yours, and what really sucks is that I don't think I would have fallen for you if you weren't so giving."

She smiled as if she'd just realized what he was saying. He wanted to kick himself.

"Jed, are you saying you'd be okay with me working from here?"

He shook his head. "I'm saying I couldn't say no because I love you too much, but, Diana, I won't share you. I know that's selfish of me, and I don't care—but yeah, I'm saying we'll give it a try."

She threw her arms around his neck and leaped up to kiss him. "Jed, thank you! You won't regret this. We'll make it work. You'll see."

He was sensing something he couldn't put into words, though. He knew no matter what she believed, in the end, something could and would create distance in place of the closeness they now shared.

Chapter 5

Diana knew Jed wouldn't be happy about her taking on work, but she also knew he'd never stand in her way and prevent her from practicing law. That kind of love was something she reminded herself she couldn't take for granted. She wanted this life with Jed, but she also wanted to be able to use her brain and dig her teeth into legal advice, papers, and research, which excited her in ways she'd forgotten.

After dropping off the boys at kindergarten and preschool, she stopped at the grocery store and tacked up a paper for her legal services, along with her phone number, and after a quick stop at the post office, where she did the same on the community bulletin where everyone posted all manner of announcements, she drove back home and pulled in beside half a dozen vehicles and a hopping class of kids and excitement.

She spied Jed leading two horses into the arena, and he stopped and waited for her. She jogged over in her sneakers, blue jeans, and the light blue shirt she'd pulled on before taking the boys in. "Hey, you. Can I help?" she said. She loved this part of Jed and what he did for these kids. It had been her passion that became his reason for doing it.

He handed her a set of reins on one of the two saddled horses. The horse nickered, rubbing his nose on her shoulder, and she followed Jed into the arena, where the kids and staff were waiting. Parents were mingling, and the energy was so happy.

"Good turnout today," Jed said. "Sherry said we have another fifteen on a waitlist. Was thinking about hiring one more to work with the horses and the kids." He had his hand on the small of her back, leading her from the arena. She loved what he did here, and he rested his forearms on the edge of the fence and looked on, smiling.

She couldn't resist leaning in and linking her arm through his, kissing his shoulder.

He glanced her way, watching her from under the shadow of his tan cowboy hat. She reached up and brushed her fingers over the shag on his face. He still hadn't shaved, but he could pull it off better than most men could.

"What?" he said, giving her an odd look.

"I'm just enjoying this. I stopped and posted some flyers, so I'm waiting to see what comes of it." She couldn't remember feeling so good, so light, in a long time. For a minute, when his expression appeared pensive, she started to worry again. "You're not going to change your mind?"

"I want you to be happy, Diana. That's all I want."

"So you're not still worried this will take time from you?"

Maybe it was the way she said it that had him

standing up, facing her, and then leaning on his elbow to look down on her. "Maybe I'm selfish, but I'm also probably the most old fashioned in our bunch. I don't think you really understand. I'm worried you're going to take on too much, because I know you and that heart of yours. You care too much. You invest all of yourself in whatever you do. I know a lot of folks look to take advantage of that generosity. You'll work yourself to the bone, and I don't want you so exhausted and tied up in knots helping others that there's nothing left for us."

It would be so easy to promise him that wouldn't happen. Although she wanted to do more, she didn't like having him point out what she already knew. "I'll promise you this, Jed: I won't take on more than I can handle. I'll make a point of shutting things down so I'm only working when the boys aren't here during the day." As she said it, for a moment, she worried it would be a promise she wouldn't be able to keep.

Maybe Jed did, too, as he turned away and said something to one of the workers before looking long and hard back at her. "I hope so, Diana, for all our sakes."

<hr>

Chapter 6

<hr>

"Who was on the phone?" she asked Jed without looking up from where she was going through her stacks of legal paper and pens, making sure all her supplies were in order in her desk. The small office at the back of the house had a large window that filled the room with light, and she shared it with Jed to run the ranch.

"Mom," he said. "She and Dad are on their way back to visit after staying with Neil and then Brad. They're staying here for a few days and then flying back to Cancun."

Diana glanced up at Jed, now understanding his expression, which seemed a little off. "Are you okay?"

He shrugged. "She's my mom still, Diana. The other stuff that happened shouldn't matter."

He was right. It shouldn't. Becky always had been a strong support, but knowing this about her past was unsettling.

"Jed, she's your mom, and Becky has always made sure I was welcome. I know it's not a good thing, but it was a long time ago. For me, I plan to put it out of my head, or try to. I'd never want your mom to know that I know. I can only imagine how hurt and disgraced she would feel if she had any idea we knew her secret. There are some things we shouldn't know about people. What I went through as a child and growing up, the shame I've had to learn to deal with, even though it wasn't my own doing…"

He was watching her with a crooked smile. "You surprise me, Diana. I was pretty wrecked hearing about it, never seen Dad so upset. Hearing my parents weren't as perfect as I believed they were, flawed like so many others, it was hard."

"Maybe that's why your mom is so understanding, because she's done things many have, but she's become a better person for it. Push comes to shove, Jed, your mom and dad will always be there for all of us, and I don't want her feeling badly or sensing we're uncomfortable."

He stepped closer inside the room, striding to her until she had to look up at him. He slid his hand around her bottom and pulled her closer to him. She could feel all his hardness. His arms were so strong and solid, and she loved being held in them.

He leaned down and was about to kiss her but stopped just short of touching his lips to hers. "Do you have time?" He tilted his head, his eyelids heavy, and she couldn't stop her hand from reaching up and skimming over the soft beard he'd started and running her thumb over his bottom lip. He nipped at the pad of her thumb with his teeth. She could feel all of him as he held her against him, his erection pushing into her stomach.

"If I said no?" she said teasingly.

He stilled for a minute. "Then I'd be mighty uncomfortable." He was watching her, and she wondered whether he thought she'd consider pushing him away.

She slid her hands around his neck and was on her tiptoes, kissing him. It didn't take long for that kiss to go from slow and easy to rough. He was tasting her until she had to fight for air amid the desire.

She couldn't speak, as he was lifting her, and she wrapped her legs around his waist as he walked them into the bedroom. He was pulling at her clothes until he had her naked under him, his own clothes tossed in a heap on the floor with them.

It was afternoon, still light out, and she couldn't remember having time to just play with her husband like this. He ran his hand over her breasts, giving them a little extra attention as he put his mouth to them. She nearly came off the bed. He was driving her a little crazy and incoherent.

"Jed, please, I want you inside me," she said with a groan, trying to reach for him, but he was having none of that as he pulled away, going lower.

"You're just going to have to be patient," he said as he kissed her stomach and hips. She tried to reach for him again, to take him in her hand, but he pressed her hands above her head, holding them there. Then he allowed his gaze to take her in, a slow lazy smile washing over his lips. "Man, are you beautiful."

When he entered her slow and easy, with long deep strokes, it felt so naughty because of the time of day and because of Jed, who seemed more attentive than usual. But loving him, being with him, and connecting with him this way filled every part of her with passion that made her believe this was why she always felt so complete—complete in a way no one else could make her feel. He touched his lips to hers, his tongue to hers, tasting her fast and furious, driving into her harder and faster while holding her still. She screamed his name, and he swore crudely and said her name again as he filled her with his warmth, spilling his seed into her and collapsing on top of her.

She wrapped her arms around his back, her legs around his waist, loving his weight on her, still buried inside her. "Just so you know, that was definitely a yes," she said.

Chapter 7

Jed was still damp from the shower he'd shared with his wife before she raced out the door to pick up the boys. He was barefoot and bare chested in the kitchen, wearing a pair of jeans that hung low on his hips as he put the roast in the oven. At least he could do that much for Diana, considering he'd basically hijacked her afternoon, bedding her and loving her as if he'd not had sex in forever. There was something about being inside her, touching her, kissing her, just feeling her that made him feel more alive than he could put into words.

Having her here with him when he was working their ranch, taking a group out for a ride, or leading a class was something he'd come to expect. He couldn't explain to anyone the joy of knowing Diana was home waiting for him. It was selfish, he understood that, but he didn't believe he could be happy fighting for scraps of time in a busy lawyer's schedule. Spending a few hours making love with his wife over and over, he knew he had a very real chance of getting her pregnant again, and that would toss out the door any chance of her working part time or doing legal work for anyone. He really was a bastard.

He heard a vehicle and the crunch of gravel, but it didn't sound like Diana's SUV, and she hadn't been gone long enough to make it back this soon, anyway. He glanced out the large picture window, seeing his mom and dad, this time driving a white Lincoln.

He had the door open by the time his dad had finished helping his mom out of the car. She was dressed smartly in light pants and a striped sweater. Her short white hair was neat and styled as it always was.

"Diana home?" she asked as she started up the steps.

Jed reached for his mom's arm and helped her up the last step. "No, she left a little bit ago to get the boys. Good to see you again as you make your travels between my brothers. How was your visit?"

"Jed, going to take the bags up to the loft!" his dad called out, lifting the suitcases from the trunk. He was dressed in dark jeans and a maroon knit shirt. He started toward the barn, where Jed had turned the loft into a very comfortable suite with a kitchen, a full bath, and two beds. It was a great place for his parents when they came to visit, which was beginning to be more frequent since his mom had had her stroke.

His mom patted his bare chest. "Maybe it was a good thing we stopped for lunch on the road. Wouldn't want to interrupt you now." She obviously knew what he'd been up to with his wife.

"I just didn't have a chance to throw a shirt on, is all," he said.

His mom went into the kitchen, filled the kettle with water, and flicked it on.

"So how about your visit with Emily, Candy, and the kids?" Jed said.

His mom rested her hand on the wooden straight-back dining chair. "It was good. Spent some time at Neil's this time out, as I feel like we spend all our time at Brad and Emily's. Theirs is a house with a lot of memories, and sometimes it seems as if we're coming home. Other times I have to remind myself it's not ours anymore."

His mom sounded a little off, and he wasn't sure why. She forced a smile, patted his arm, and wandered into the small front room, the one he still had plans to add on to, bringing it out to double the size of the living room, maybe build a separate dining room. Then, they already had the addition in back with a family room and an extra bedroom. More kids would mean more rooms. He smiled to himself.

"You seem pretty pleased with yourself," Becky said. The rocking chair creaked as she lowered her plump body into it. She was wearing the same dark shoes with orthotics that she always wore of late. Her face was pale, and her eyes didn't have that sparkle she always carried whenever she was around her family.

"You okay, Mom?"

She waved her hand as he leaned on the back of the sofa. "Just tired. Didn't sleep well the last few nights. That's why I said to your father it was time to come to your place, and then I think we'll head back home to Cancun before the weather turns."

"It's still early, Mom. Nights are getting cooler, but it's fall. I thought you enjoyed spending time with your grandkids." Now he was starting to feel bad, knowing her secret and wondering whether she had any idea that they knew.

She didn't say anything for a moment. What was going through his mom's head? It was as if she was somehow aware that her secret was no longer that. He hoped not, anyway. Maybe it was time to speak with his dad.

"Of course I do, but I don't want to wear out our welcome," she said. "Besides, I remember the days of back-to-school chaos, getting you boys ready and out the door on the bus. Emily has her hands full, and Brad, too. But it was Neil. I wonder if he's happy, living where he's living and giving up everything, his resort, his deals, for a simple life in that small Washington community."

"Did he say something?" Jed said. He wondered, too, about everything Neil had walked away from, considering he was the brother who had always done everything on a grand scale. His motto had always been "Go big or go home."

"Didn't have to. I know you boys so well, your moods, and I understand when something is unsettled in each of you. He's lucky, though. He has Candy, and she balances him in a way he needs. But he's also at a point in his life where he needs to decide which road he's going to take, and I see him stumbling a bit. I've been there. You recognize that part of life we all get to, some more than others, where we question everything, the choices we made, the mistakes, what we can live with and what we don't want to continue. He just needs some time, some space. He didn't need us underfoot." She waved her hand, but Jed wasn't so sure. Out of all of them, Neil had been most put out to hear the secret, considering Candy had already known and never told him.

Maybe Neil had said something and that was why they were back so early. He wanted a word with his brother. Maybe he'd call him later, speak to him, because the last thing any of them should be doing was making their mother feel unwelcome. "Stay as long as you want," Jed said. "You and Dad are always welcome. I know it's good for Diana having you around."

His mom smiled again as if he'd said exactly what she needed to hear. "Everything all right?"

"Just some things. Her mom came around again. Seems she was here before and Diana didn't tell me."

His mom just rocked in the chair, resting her hands over her stomach. "That doesn't sound too good. What does this woman want with Diana?"

"That's the thing. I'm not really sure, and that's what bothers me. She came in here saying she needs to make amends, leaving a pamphlet from a recovering addicts group that meets in town. But I can't shake this feeling she's up to something more, considering I warned her off and she's made it clear she's not going to listen."

"How's Diana feeling about this? I'm sure it can't be easy, not having that maternal love growing up. I can only imagine what it's doing to her, having her showing up and maybe saying all the things she wants to hear— things she needs to hear."

What could his mother be thinking? Diana was fine. She had him and the boys, and his parents were hers. She also knew that Brad, Neil, and Andy would have her back. She had to know, so why was his mother hinting at something else?

"Jed, I can tell by that look that you don't really understand, and maybe there's more going on?"

"I don't get it, with Diana, why she let her mom come back here. Why didn't she tell me? Now she has this idea of working again."

His mom now appeared amused as she really looked at him. "Jed Friessen, you're married to a brilliant, kind woman who's sharp as a whip, and she chose you and her boys over a career in law. That should say something to you. She should work. It would be good for her to start practicing law, something else she loves to do, instead of squandering everything on you."

He could feel his neck warm as he stepped back, crossing his arms over his bare chest, wondering what had gotten into his mom.

She waved her hand in the air at him. "Don't give me that done-wrong look, Jed. You're as bad as Neil sometimes. Sometimes a woman has to have something other than just her husband, home, and children, something else that stirs her passion and makes her happy. A happy woman is a happy wife. You don't want to take that from her. You listen to me on this, because I know."

Now she was making him sound like an ass. He wanted Diana happy, but he also wanted to be the one to bring her joy. "Mom, she's happy here!" He gestured to the floor. "At home."

His mom raised an eyebrow and then laughed at him.

"Well, she will be," he said. "She just needs to be busy again." This time, he didn't miss the odd expression on his mom's face as if she'd figured out what he was up to.

"Oh, Jed, really? You're not suggesting what I think you are."

He wasn't sure he wanted to answer that, considering he didn't know what his mom was thinking, so he said nothing as the front door opened and his dad walked in, taking in the two of them.

"What's going on?" Rodney asked.

His mom rocked, pressing both hands on the arms of the chair, and said, "Your son here thinks getting his wife pregnant will get any thought of working as a lawyer again out of her head. Isn't that right, Jed?"

His dad didn't say a word, just stared at his mom.

"Diana loves children, and what's wrong with having another baby?" Jed said. Why did it sound so wrong coming out of his mouth?

"Jed, there's nothing wrong with having another baby, but if your intention is to saddle Diana down with a brood of children so she has no room in her life for a career that inspires her, well, you're headed down a one-way road to disaster," Becky said. "You can't take something from someone you love because you want all of her. It's not okay, Jed, because what'll happen is that something inside Diana will slowly die. If you really understood what you were doing and the repercussions, I'd think you'd let Diana make the choice, and maybe you'd help her so there'd be room in your life for both."

He listened to the sound of Diana driving in with his boys in the SUV, and he watched through the window as she walked around the vehicle to open the back door and help the boys out, listening to the chatter of excitement from his kids. He couldn't help feeling like a selfish ass as he took in the joy and light in his wife's face, her eyes sparkling like they hadn't in months when she hugged his dad and his mom.

When his dad's gaze lingered on him as he lifted Christopher and hugged him, Jed realized that for the first time, Rodney and Becky weren't on the same page.

Chapter 8

"I'm so glad you and Rodney made it back," Diana said. "The boys are always so excited to see their grandparents, and I have to admit it gives me a break."

Becky was peeling potatoes while Diana rinsed off broccoli. She was glad it had been easy to remind herself how much she loved being with Jed's mom. Becky was such a warm, vibrant woman who truly cared about all of them.

"Jed said your mom came back." Becky dropped a peeled potato in a pot of water before glancing her way.

For a minute, Diana was stuck on what to say. Damn Jed for saying anything. "She did. I'm sure Jed also told you I didn't tell him about the other times she showed up." She took a breath. There had been no excuse except for the fact that when he had come riding in on his horse both times, she had meant to say something but had stopped because she was so confused about the things her mother had said.

"He did mention that part. I can't imagine what

you're feeling. I had wonderful parents who were loving and together and solid, and when I think of what you went through, what you didn't have, my heart aches." She continued peeling another potato, staring down at it. "What is it she wants, Diana? I mean, Jed warned her not to come back, and I know my sons are not the kind of men smart people ignore a warning from."

"I guess that's one thing about my mother I've always known. She's not the kind who listens or would ever consider doing the right thing. But to answer your question, I don't really know what she wants. She says she wants to make amends, even brought along this pamphlet about some recovery group she's part of." She stared down at the broccoli head and set it on the cutting board.

"So she wants you to go, and what?" Becky asked.

When she glanced over at her mother-in-law, she realized she didn't really understand either. "I don't know, and maybe that's what scares me. Even though deep down inside of me I want it to be real, for her to be sorry and really want to make amends, to make things right with me, to think that maybe she could be trying to be better, at the same time I'm afraid it's all a sham and she's still the same awful person." Her voice cracked.

Becky didn't say a thing as she reached over and touched Diana's hand, giving it a gentle squeeze and then a pat before she started cutting up the potatoes into chunks. "I suppose that sounds about right, but don't be afraid to find out, Diana."

She glanced over at Becky, wondering what she was getting at. "I don't think Jed would want me digging around too much in my mother's direction, and I understand why. He's always trying to protect me." She smiled because she'd never felt so safe as when she knew he had her back, her strong, overly protective alpha husband.

"My son, like his brothers, can be a little overbearing. There are just some things you need to find out. Don't get me wrong, and just so we're clear, I do agree with my son on one thing: You shouldn't be alone with your mother. You may always be vulnerable there, and if she's up to something…" She stopped talking as if she were thinking.

"I'm not sure I understand what you're talking about. I'm pretty sure everyone in the family, Rodney, Brad, Neil, Andy, Candy, and Emily, too, were all dead set on my mother coming around here."

"Oh, we are, but this…" Becky lifted the brochure piled with other mail and papers on the edge of the counter. "This is filled with a lot of questions, like this Thursday's support group meeting your mother mentioned. Well, maybe it's time we find out what's really going on."

She stared over at the light blue brochure that she'd glanced through and put down, because she knew Jed wouldn't in a million years be okay with her stopping in at her mother's meeting. "Jed wouldn't like it."

"Maybe not, but how about tomorrow, you and I go?"

"Go where?" Jed said. Diana hadn't heard him come in, and he lifted off his hat and set it on the back of the chair. He was sweating as he stared down at his mom and over to her.

"To my mother's meeting in town," Diana said.

Jed didn't even bat an eye, staring at her as if she'd lost her mind. Then, slowly, he looked down at his mom, who put the lid on the pot of potatoes and put it on the stove, flicking on the burner.

"I think it's a fine idea," Becky said. "And, Jed, just so you're not worried, I'll go with Diana, find out what this woman's story really is, and you can look after the kids."

Jed said nothing, but the look that passed between Becky and her son spoke volumes. Something more was going on between them.

Chapter 9

Jed cut open another bale of hay, dropping some inside each of the stalls for the eight horses he'd already brought in for the night. Their stalls had been cleaned and their water buckets filled. He heard the clatter of footsteps on the stairs coming down from the loft, and when the door opened, his dad appeared. Rodney was tall, his white hair recently cut, wearing a green cable-knit sweater and blue jeans.

"Hi, Dad. Is Mom settled in okay?" Jed said.

"She just turned in. She's tired. Need some help?" Rodney asked, taking a pair of work gloves from the bin beside the tack room.

"Sure, if you can toss the hay to those three on the end, then I think we're done."

His dad grabbed an armful of hay and tossed some in each of the stalls.

"Is there something else going on with Mom?"

Rodney pulled off the work gloves and tossed them back in the bin. "In what way are you asking?"

"Well, you heard she's encouraging Diana to meet

with Faye, and she plans to go with her. I remember a time not too long ago when she was more focused on me making sure Diana's mother never set foot near her again." He was still pissed at the fact that his mother seemed ready to stir things up when he was doing his best to try to settle them down.

"In this, I probably agree with your mother. From what I heard, anyway, I think your mom wants to have a chance to size up the woman who all but tossed Diana away. Secondly, it's about forgiveness."

Was his dad serious? "Some things just aren't forgivable, Dad. You should know that."

Rodney was shaking his head, looking pretty grim. "No, you don't get it, Jed, and maybe it took your mother and me a lifetime to learn this, but holding on to anger is only hurting you. You're not forgiving just to say that it's okay or to welcome her back into your life. You're forgiving to release yourself, and maybe your mom is right. This is about Diana needing to let that part of her life go, and forgiving her mother is maybe what she needs to do to move on and put it behind her."

"I don't want Faye anywhere near Diana, or messing with her." Jed was trying to get his dad to understand.

Rodney gestured toward him, leaning against the stall door. "Nor do I, and I think your mom is smart enough to figure out whether this woman has an agenda or is truly trying to make amends."

Jed didn't like it, and he yanked his own gloves off before shoving them in his back pocket.

"Just so you know, Jed, your mother is very much in support of Diana having something more than just you and the boys. I'm going to say this, so understand me: What we think doesn't matter. Just don't make the mistakes I did. We love Diana, she's a wonderful mother and daughter-in-law, and we want to see her as happy as you. Maybe I understand the part of you that wants to keep her pregnant and busy with your kids so you have all of her here, but stifling her, making her be here only for you and the boys and give up everything just to be a wife and mother, isn't fair to her. Even though my first instinct was to be very much on your side, Diana is different than your mother, Jed."

He had to look away because he knew his dad was right, but he also knew how unhappy he'd be if he had to fight for pieces of his wife's time or if she exhausted herself so much that she'd have no time to be a wife and mother. It would slowly destroy their family.

"Diana knew when she married me that I wanted a family and a stay-at-home mother, with my kids not stuck in a daycare." Jed watched his father raise his eyebrows as if he needed a reality check.

"Times change, Jed. You can't expect to stick her here on the ranch and for her to forget everything else of who she is and who she wants to be. I heard it's a little time every week she's asking for, not all the time, and there's a difference."

Now it was Jed's turn to be surprised at how enlightened his father sounded.

"I'm quoting your mother, by the way, but I happen to believe for the most part that she's right. Diana's your wife, but she's a part of our family, Jed, so you need to figure out how to balance family, your wife, and happiness. I can't do that for you, and neither can your mother. You need to do that yourself." The quiet lingered, and a horse nickered softly when his dad made a move, tapping the stall door. "Well, I'm going to turn in. Good night, son." Rodney lingered for a moment and then rested his hand on Jed's shoulder before pulling open the door that led up to the loft.

Jed stood there, listening to his father's footsteps before shutting off the lights and closing up the barn door. As he took in the light shining through the front window, he wished everything could go back to how it had been with Diana. He loved her so much, and the reality was that no matter how selfish he wanted to be, he couldn't and wouldn't keep something she loved from her. No matter what, his dad was right. He was going to have to find a way to make it work.

Chapter 10

The entire ride into town, Diana could feel the effects of the night before with Jed, then again this morning, as he had woken her by rolling her over, spreading her legs, and slipping inside her. It had been a while since he'd made love to her to the degree he was now. He'd taken her three times before she'd fallen asleep, leaving her feeling him and the part of himself he had left inside her still.

"I think Jed is trying to get me pregnant again," she said to Becky, who was sitting in the front passenger seat. For a second, she felt her face heat when her mother-in-law smiled.

"Men," she said with a chuckle. "My sons, much like their father, believe having a baby and adding another child is all that is needed to settle a woman."

She should be mad at Jed, but instead all she felt was conflicted.

"It's none of my business, Diana, but tell me, would it be so horrible?" Becky was watching her as she glanced back to the highway, thinking for a minute.

Finally, she shook her head. "No, how could it be? It's just that I'd like to have some time for me right now, because having a baby, I would need to be there all the time. Don't get me wrong, I wouldn't hate it. Actually, I would love it. I would love every minute of being there, holding and loving my baby."

"Maybe that daughter you've always wanted," Becky added.

Diana wondered how she knew. "There's something special about the mother–daughter relationship that I want to have. I love my boys and every minute with them, but when Laura and Andy were here with that beautiful, sweet baby girl…I wanted a daughter so bad."

The silence was thick, and it lingered as she stayed with that thought.

"I know and understand, Diana. You're talking to a woman who had three boys. A daughter would have been nice." For a moment, Becky sounded so wistful, and she said nothing else as Diana pulled into the half-full parking lot of an old church in the center of town.

The red brick was crumbling in spots. A few people were crossing to the cement stairs leading to the basement, and Diana found herself trying to picture what each person was here for. What were their stories?

"So are we going to sit here the entire meeting, or are we going in?" Becky asked from where she sat in the passenger seat, wearing sunglasses to keep the brightness from the late-day sun from her eyes. "Doesn't matter much to me. If you're not ready, I can just sit here with you, or we can go home."

"Back to Jed, to tell him I was too scared to go in," Diana said. She couldn't do that even though she knew he'd understand. He'd most likely be happy, too, since he really hadn't wanted her coming in the first place, but she had to cut him some slack because he was beginning to surprise her with his support in places she'd never expected. She loved him so much for that, because he was trying to understand her need to achieve for herself, to face her demons. Diana also realized how much Jed was having to put aside his feelings for her to have something for herself. It was so unselfish, and if she'd ever had any doubt about the depth of her husband's love, she didn't now.

Her hands were still gripping the steering wheel, and she glanced down at her husband's ring on her finger and rubbed it. She looked over to Becky, who was watching her with an expression that said she understood some of Diana's anxiety.

"Well, I guess we better go in," Diana said. She opened her door to go around to the passenger side, but Becky was already climbing down. With arms linked, they walked into the basement of the church.

The meeting was already in progress when she guided Becky to two seats in back.

"Is she here?" Becky whispered to her, and a man in front turned and shushed them.

Diana glanced around the room, where at least twenty people were sitting. There were six double rows of five chairs, each with empty spots here and there between attendees. She glanced over to an older balding man and spotted her mother's vibrant red hair. Today she had worn it down, long and lush, those familiar locks in the second row from the front. Faye was sitting in between two men, and as Diana glanced around at the people, she was surprised to see Carl Furness, the long-time manager of the Butcher's Block, one of the fancier all-beef restaurants in these parts, sitting beside her. She wondered what addiction he had: alcohol, drugs, gambling, sex? She listened to one woman up front talk about her downfall into internet porn. She was a former kindergarten teacher who had lost everything, her job, husband, home, and family, along with her dignity. The group clapped with support for the woman speaking about something so humiliating and private.

Diana leaned closer to Becky and pointed out her mother. Becky nodded and reached for her hand when Faye Claremont stood up and took a place at the front. She was dressed in a short-sleeved white blouse and black pencil skirt. She still had an amazing figure, and Diana supposed she could pull off wearing anything and still make it look sexy. She smiled brightly, scanning the crowd until her gaze stopped on Diana, where it lingered for a second. She took in Becky beside her before clearing her throat.

"Hello, my name is Faye."

Diana listened to everyone call out a welcome, and for a minute she wondered what her mother was going to say.

"This is very difficult for me to stand up here and share with everyone." She glanced back over to Diana and held her gaze quite intently. It was unnerving, and she had to swallow, recognizing the determination there. It reminded her of a time when her mother couldn't be reasoned with. She'd always had her mind made up, and no one or nothing was ever going to change it. She was a strong woman with a strong mind and a destructive soul.

She felt Becky reach for her hand and give it a squeeze. Maybe she realized Diana's mom had zeroed in on her.

"I was ten years old when a seventeen-year-old sharing my foster home raped me. I was just one of twelve kids shoved in that home, a check for the people running it. I had no one to talk to, no one to turn to, and by the time I turned sixteen, I'd lost count of the number of men I'd been with, not understanding the difference between, sex, love, and abuse. It became blurred, and so did the faces and the names. There were teachers, other teenage boys who showed up in the foster home, an uncle of my foster mom, a neighbor. I never wondered at any time what it was they saw in me that made them believe I was an easy target. Then one of them gave me pills, I don't remember who, because everything and everyone began to blur into one until I couldn't tell one man from the other, one moment from the next. The pills gave way to booze, to whatever drug was available. I had my first child at eighteen, and another was born not right in the head several years later. She died."

The way she said it had Diana tearing up, remembering Louisa, the sister she'd cared for and looked after, doing her best at nine years old to protect her from her mother, an angry drunk.

"There are a lot of things I'm ashamed of, horrible things I did that I need to make amends for. Even though I am a victim, it was my daughter who suffered, not having a mother to look after her because I spent my nights drunk at the bars, selling drugs, partying and sleeping with whoever was going to pay my way. I soon learned that I could use what all men had taken from me for my benefit, and I capitalized on it. But soon those things came to an end. One night, I was so desperate after being thrown out of the only home we had. I was with my girls, sitting in my car. I stopped at a bar and picked the wrong guy to sell drugs to—or he could have been the right one, depending on how you look at it. He was an undercover cop.

"I was arrested and sentenced to ten years. After five

years of hell, I finally opened up my heart and started to heal." She took a breath, still watching Diana, and everyone was quiet and waiting. "I hurt a lot of people. I did a lot of bad things. I'm an alcoholic and am addicted to sex. After my release from prison, I floundered lost for a long while. I was sober for a lot of years, but I slipped again when I got out. I've been sober now for thirty-five months." She smiled at everyone. "I'd like to thank my baby for being here today and for forgiving me." She gestured to Diana.

There were claps and cheers, and Diana felt for a moment as if she'd been sucker punched.

"Mighty presumptuous," Becky said in a low voice.

Diana couldn't speak. No way had she said she'd forgiven her, and she took exception to that. She wanted to leave, but she couldn't get her legs to move, so she stayed in that hard plastic chair as two more people got up to speak. Diana didn't hear a word they said, knowing her mother was stealing glances her way. She wanted nothing more than to get out of there, but then everyone was standing up, chairs were scraping, and people were talking. Faye appeared when she finally stood and helped Becky up.

"I'm so glad you came," Faye said, smiling, and then reached out and touched Diana's arm. She was so stiff and was glad the moment Becky reached for her hand again and squeezed.

"I'm Becky Friessen," she said, which was helpful, since Diana's tongue had thickened and she couldn't get it to move, let alone get one word out.

"Oh, well, you're Jed's mother? Nice to meet you. I'm Faye Claremont. I'm so glad you came, Diana. It makes me so happy that you'll give me the opportunity to make things right with you."

"So what are your intentions with Diana, Faye?" Becky asked. Diana had to glance her way, a little surprised at the bluntness but also grateful. It was something she should have thought of.

"Well, she's my daughter, and not a day has passed that I haven't thought of her or how she's doing. I need to make amends. It's part of the steps of recovery, but it's more than that. I never got the chance to see my baby grow up. She was taken from me." She sounded so sad for a moment.

Hearing her emotion left Diana feeling torn and slipping again. It was as if her mother knew exactly how to reel her in, so she gave her head a shake, reminding herself that her mother always spoke and acted with such dramatics. She heard Becky sigh.

"Faye, I came to hear you—"

"Please, Diana, I'm Mama to you," Faye said, cutting her off before she could finish. For a moment, she remembered how often that tone would be followed by a stinging slap across the face, and she had to back up.

"You're not my mother. Let me be clear on that." Who was this strong, reasonable person she sounded like? How she wished for a moment that Jed had come. "I had wonderful foster parents."

Becky squeezed her hand again, maybe giving her support. "I may be Jed's mother," she said, "but Diana is my daughter, too, after marrying into our family. You want to make amends, and that's good, but you're not her mother. I'm also not clear on a few things. Why did you come back to this town, to this place, where there could be no future for you?"

For a moment, Faye appeared flustered. "Diana came back here. It's where Diana lives, and I can't make things right if I'm not here."

Okay, she had to give her mother that, maybe.

"Tell me, what are your goals for the future?" Becky asked. Diana found herself looking between Faye and Becky, who both seemed to be talking around her. How easy would it be to just slip out the door if Becky weren't holding her hand? It struck her from out of nowhere, punching her in the chest until the ache expanded. This was what she'd always done with her mother when she was on a rampage: sneak away before she got hit.

"Goals, well, I want to have a relationship with my daughter. She has children, and I'd like to get to know them. She's my only family."

"Hmm, and you work, have a job?" Becky asked.

"Well, yes. I'm waiting tables, make good tips. It's a start and pays the bills. I'm limited on what I can get, having a record. It's hard. The first box you check on a job application is whether you've been convicted of a felony, and I can't lie. I'm just lucky that a good man like Carl Furness gave me a chance."

Diana didn't want to look up, because now she wondered whether Carl was here for Faye. She really didn't want to know much more. "Okay, then," she said. "You know what? I need to go. We need to go." She was flustered and felt her face heat as she looked down at Becky.

"Oh, Diana, please, before you go, I want you to meet Carl." Faye put her hand on Diana's arm, a touch she didn't want, because it wasn't warm and nurturing. Then Faye was waving at someone, and Carl appeared beside her, smiling and then glancing over, looking hopefully at Diana. He had gray hair and brown eyes, was of regular height and build, and had lines on his face that made him seem older than what she thought he was, a man in his early to mid fifties.

"Faye, we do need to go." Becky leaned in, sliding her hand around Diana's waist, maybe realizing her need to get away from this.

Then Carl was standing in her way, blocking her exit.

"Carl, this is my daughter, Diana," Faye said.

He held out his hand. "Diana, we've met, but I have to say, wow, you're stunning, just like your mother. How is Jed?"

She took his hand, shook it, and pulled away, reaching back to touch Becky's arm. "Good. He's waiting for me at home, and we need to get going."

She started to step around her mother and Carl, but Faye sidestepped them, putting both her hands up to Diana's forearms to stop her. It was a move that seemed so desperate.

"Please wait," she said. "There's something really important I need to talk to you about."

"Faye, please, we need to go." She didn't want to listen to this, and she was also of the mind that Jed was right. He hadn't wanted her coming here, and now she wished she would have listened.

"Diana, please, just five minutes. This is really important. I know you're busy, but Carl is my friend…"

"Faye, look, don't," Carl said. "It's fine. I can find someone else to help. Don't push your daughter."

What was this about? She didn't like it and felt Becky tighten her arm around her.

"No, Carl. Please, Diana," her mother pleaded. "Carl has been a good friend to me. He gave me a job when no one else would, and you being a lawyer and all, you could help him. Carl saw your flyer in the grocery store. You're looking for work. He can give you some. Please, I told him you're a lawyer, and my baby is really good at what she does."

"So this is about Diana being a lawyer. Is that why you wanted her to come?" Becky asked, and she didn't sound at all pleased.

"No. I need to make amends with Diana, that much is true, but Carl has a situation that he needs someone to help him with. It's delicate."

She wanted to roll her eyes. "Delicate" meant he'd gotten his hand caught in the cookie jar and needed someone good to help extract it. "Seriously?" she muttered, looking down at Becky and then back at Faye, wondering now, if she listened, would Faye in fact go away and leave her alone? The thought both saddened and relieved her.

"Faye, that's about enough," Becky said, pushing between them. "Diana, let's go."

"It's okay, Becky," Diana said. "I'll give you five minutes. You tell me what it is you want my help with, and I'll listen, but I'm not promising anything. Then I'm going to walk away."

"Deal," Faye said, glancing hopefully in Carl's direction, and it was evident in that exchange that there was a relationship there—one Diana wanted to know nothing about.

She gestured to the corner away from everyone, and Faye smiled brightly as Becky said to her, "I don't think this is a good idea. Jed will not like this."

No, he wouldn't, but she also knew that until she heard her mother out, the woman was not going to go away.

Chapter 11

The colors in the western sky were a brilliant orange and red as the sun set. It was the time of year when the lazy hot days of summer were over and the cool nights of fall were arriving. Harvests were being brought in, and the summer rush of overnight and day horseback riding trips was over until the spring. Fall always gave way to slowing down and spending more time with family, his boys, and Diana. It was a time of year he really looked forward to.

"Daddy, when's Mommy coming home?" Christopher asked for what felt like the tenth time in an hour. Of course he missed Diana. She was always here for the boys and for him. She was their rock, grounding this family.

He picked up his dark-haired little boy and patted his bottom, hugging him. "Soon, she just went in to town with Grandma. Why don't you go get your pajamas on? Then let's get your teeth brushed for bed."

"But I can't go to sleep till Mommy comes home.

Mommy always kisses me goodnight before bed. I can't sleep if she doesn't kiss me."

Jed sighed. This was only the first of many nights when Diana would be late or working, and Christopher was too young to understand that grownups sometimes just couldn't be there. Jed didn't want his boys aching for an absent mother.

He put Christopher down. "It's just one night, Christopher," he said to remind himself. "Go on, get your teeth brushed, and then you can pick out a book to read." He was hoping to distract his son as he watched Danny come jumping down the hall, Rodney behind him.

"This one was just showing me all he learned at school today, all his artwork." Rodney loved his grandkids and spent more quality time with them than he had spent with Brad, Neil, and Jed when they were growing up.

"I want to show Mom. When is she coming back?" Danny had a light smattering of freckles on his face, and his red hair had a natural wave that made it look as if he hadn't brushed it. It was more that he needed a haircut.

"You can show your mom when she gets home. Now, no more asking where she is. She'll be home soon…"

He heard the sound of a vehicle coming, and he didn't need to look to know it was his wife. He knew the sound of her car just like the sound of her footsteps. He breathed a sigh of relief, realizing he had been as thrown as the boys at Diana not being there. "Diana's home. None too soon," he said to his dad.

The boys were ecstatic, and Christopher pulled open the door, racing out and leaping into Diana's arms as she came around the front of the SUV. Then Danny was there, both trying to talk to Diana at once, telling her everything, all of it dramatic, that had happened that day.

As he watched his wife with their little boys, the love, the worry, and the fact that they had all of her in those few seconds, he realized Diana needed her children as much as they needed her, and the tightness in his shoulders, back, and chest eased a bit more.

She stopped beside him in the chaos, offering her lips for him to kiss. He slid his hand over her cheek and gave her a quick soft kiss while she carried Christopher, his arms around her neck, legs around her waist, as if he were a toddler still.

"Everything okay?" he asked.

She sighed, looking first at Christopher and then Danny, who was holding her big bulky purse, and then up at Jed. She started to say something, but she stopped, looking at him as if she needed him to just hold her. Something was wrong.

"Hey, why don't you boys go in with your granddad and give your mom time to get in the door?" Jed said, looking to his dad, who maybe understood that he and Diana needed some time and space just to talk.

"Christopher, Danny, come on, both of you. Do what your dad said and brush your teeth." Rodney reached for Danny from Diana, who didn't want to let go until she kissed him, and then set him on the ground. He followed both boys down the hall.

Diana glanced back at Becky, who was walking up the stairs, holding the railing and shaking her head. "I hate to say this, Jed, but I think you were right," Diana said. His mom looked tired, not her happy, vibrant self.

"In what way? I don't think I'm liking this," Jed said as Diana pressed the flat of her hand to his chest, splaying her fingers. She wouldn't look at him as she leaned in and pressed her head to the center of his chest.

"I wish you would have come," she mumbled into his chest, turning her head to press her cheek into his chest as he slid his arm around her. She was so tight, and he rubbed her back, feeling her tension as he glanced at his mom, of course thinking all kinds of things he didn't like.

"Do you want to tell me what happened?"

Becky was shaking her head again. "You're right, she's a beautiful woman, but it's all surface. She reminds me so much of Crystal in a way."

Jed didn't like hearing Brad's ex-wife's name. She was a deceitful woman who'd torn their family apart for years. She was selfish to the bone, and Jed was grateful Brad had figured it out and found Emily.

Becky reached out to Diana and rubbed her back before starting into the house. "I'll go give Rodney a hand with my grandsons. Jed, why don't you spend some time with Diana and talk?"

The front door closed, and Diana rubbed her cheek against his shirt again as if trying to get closer to him. "I love you so much, Jed."

Of course that had him holding her closer, still not wanting to let her go. He should have gone with her. He'd wanted to, had insisted once, but for some reason he'd assumed Diana needed the space. It was the first time he hadn't pushed.

"Diana, at times I want to lock you in this house so nothing bad can touch you. It was the hardest thing for me, letting you go there alone."

She pulled away, but she didn't stop touching him. "I wasn't alone. Your mom was there, and I'm very grateful for that, but this was the first time I've walked into something from my past without you there to slay my dragons. I knew you would've. You'd have made it better. It was hard, Jed, all of it, being there, listening and not being able to say a word when I should have, and then I ached because if you had been there, you would have handled all of it, and I wanted that. Then, at the same time, I was mad at myself for not being able to stand on my own two feet."

He lifted his hand to touch her face, and she shut her eyes, pressing her cheek into his hand as if she needed to absorb the feeling.

"So tell me what happened," he said, sounding reasonable when deep down he wanted to drive in to town and raise holy hell at Faye for messing with his wife in this way. He didn't like seeing this insecurity, knowing she had needed him and he hadn't been there.

"She talked about what happened to her, bad things that messed her up to be like she was. She was molested as a child, turned to drugs and booze and sex, a victim herself. She said she wanted to make amends, that it's part of the steps. Fine, great, I said to myself, and then I wanted to get the hell out of there and come home." Her voice cracked.

"Sounds to me like she was making excuses," Jed said, and Diana appeared confused.

"I don't know. Maybe."

"No maybes, Diana. You know as well as I that a lot of people have bad things happen to them, but as an adult you have a choice to grow up and pull yourself together, and she chose to be a bad parent, to be a bad person. That was all on her, no matter what happened to her. No excuses."

Diana held up her hands and shook her head. "I get that, Jed, and I understand and agree with you. She made a choice, and now she has to live with it, but she's trying to make a new start. She's working in town, waitressing at that fancy steak place." She rested her hands on his arms again, and he was thinking of the restaurant. He'd taken Diana there a few times, but he'd make sure they went somewhere else now.

"The manager there, you know him." Diana flicked her gaze up at him.

"Yeah, Carl. Good guy, quiet. Think he had some problems a while back with gambling. Lost his family over it. What does he have to do with this?"

"He was there at the meeting. I saw him and was wondering what he was there for. Then he came over. Faye called him, said they're friends, but I think it's more."

He really wasn't sure he liked hearing her mother was making friends and building something with anyone in this town. It was too permanent, and the chances of her wanting to reconnect with Diana could and would grow. Maybe he should go and have a word with Carl.

"When I tried to leave, she stopped me, and it became clear she wanted something. It had to do with me being a lawyer, but it wasn't for her. She wanted me to help Carl."

"And you left, right? You said, 'I don't think so.' Tell me you said that."

Of course she hadn't, though. He could tell just by looking at her that she had compassion for someone who didn't deserve it.

She shook her head. "I gave her five minutes to tell me what she wanted and then to leave me alone forever."

He knew he wasn't going to like this. "So you gave her your time, and she gave you a sob story."

Diana appeared conflicted and gazed back at him. "It wasn't what I thought. I imagined a whole slew of cry-me-a-river kinds of stories, but it wasn't. He's just trying to see his son." Jed shook his head, and Diana sighed. "His ex-wife was a Canadian, and she's moved back to her hometown in Vancouver. He has two kids, both grown, but his son has ALS. He's dying and has been hooked up to machines, and that's all that's keeping him alive. Carl can't get into Canada because he has a record."

Jed didn't know Carl well, but hearing that surprised him. How well could he ever really know someone? "What did he do?"

"It was years ago, when he was gambling. He was taking money from his employer, and he got caught, copped a plea. Didn't do jail time, but he has a record for theft, and the Canadian authorities won't let him in. They do some of the most rigorous checks, going back to someone's eighteenth birthday. Felony convictions are inadmissible, even less serious offences. He's tried already and was turned down. He just wants to see his son, to say goodbye."

The one thing he had been afraid of happening was playing out, because a cause like this would have Diana doing everything she could to help this man. "Diana, I'm sorry for him, I really am, but is there no one else who could do this?"

This time she stepped away, appearing as if he'd slapped her. "Jed, there's me. I can help or at least get him started in the right direction. This is what I do. This is what it means to be a lawyer."

"Mommy, are you coming in? Can you read a story?" Christopher opened the door on his tiptoes, dressed in his blue pajamas.

"Of course. I'm coming in right now, and I'd love to read to you." She bent down and kissed his nose, then smiled as he giggled.

"Diana, seriously, let this go," Jed said. "Tell him no. You really think it's a good idea helping anyone who's friendly with your mother?"

She didn't look at him for a second as she ran her hands over Christopher's head. "I have to, Jed. I really want to help him. He just wants to see his son. This is one of the reasons I became a lawyer," she said.

Then Jed watched his wife take Christopher into the house, her mind made up, chatting and happy and laughing with her boys. As he stepped in behind her, he didn't miss his mother, who was watching him with a hint of sadness and shaking her head.

Chapter 12

She'd read through a dozen articles, legal briefs, and pieces of information, and all she could do was help Carl find a lawyer certified by any of the Canadian provinces to handle the application to Immigration Canada on grounds of compassion. It wouldn't be too difficult, considering he'd never served jail time and the offense had happened twelve years earlier. Why her mother had insisted Carl speak with her, she didn't know, but she'd buried herself in finding out everything she could to help him, including his best approach, for the past two days. Through all that, she'd done exactly what Jed had feared.

She'd ignored her family.

She dropped her pen on her desk and scooted back her chair, flicking off the lamp that provided light in the darkened room. She could hear voices in the living room and blinked as she stepped into the hallway, stopping in the doorway of Christopher's room and seeing his little leg kicked out overtop his quilt. She smiled as she stepped into his room and gently eased him back under the covers.

When she pulled the door so it was just ajar again, she felt Jed standing there so close, watching her but not touching her.

"You finish up?" he asked, setting his hands on his hips.

"All done. Sorry about dinner and the boys today."

He didn't say anything as he glanced over her head to the bedroom where her son was sleeping. Then he took her arm and pulled her into their bedroom, closing the door behind them. His hand was braced against the door, and he was looking down at the floor as if he was thinking some pretty heavy thoughts. Then he sighed before glancing over. Good grief. Her heart sank as she realized he was disappointed.

"I know what you're going to say, Jed," she said before he could begin.

He didn't say anything, just waited her out as if he wanted her to explain. She swallowed, feeling like crap, because she was torn between wanting to help Carl get to see his son one last time and missing this time with her boys, with Jed. "I took all this time from you, and I promised you I wouldn't, that I could work only when the boys are in school, but this was just a one-time thing." She stopped when his eyes sparked with an anger she hadn't seen in a while.

"Bullshit, Diana. Be honest in this, will you? It's not a one-time thing. It can never be a one-time thing with you, and I told you that from the start. You don't know how to give half. You give all of yourself."

She couldn't remember him ever sounding so mad at her. He didn't try to touch her. In fact, he walked around her and started undoing his shirt. "Okay, I get it, you're mad. I'm sorry I wasn't here for you, and I'm sorry I was so wrapped up in working."

He turned around, his shirt half undone, gesturing to the door. "Danny lost his tooth and was so excited, and you were the one he wanted to show it to, but with you so busy, reading, researching, whatever it was you were doing, you didn't even hear him when he tried to tell you this morning. You said 'That's nice' and walked away, reading whatever it was."

She touched her chest with her hand, trying to think, but she couldn't for the life of her remember. She'd been so wrapped up in reading, figuring out the steps Carl should take. She remembered getting coffee, and Jed had been there with the boys. What was wrong with her? "I'm so sorry, Jed." She put her hand to her mouth and glanced to the door, wanting to go across the hall and check on Danny.

"Don't!" Jed said. He must have known. "He's asleep. I took care of it, put money under his pillow." He pulled out the tooth from his pocket, opened the drawer of the bedside table, and tucked it inside.

"I'm sorry," Diana said. She felt it in every part of her and took a step toward her husband, who was anything but forgiving right now, as he sat down on the edge of the bed and finished unbuttoning his shirt. He had a fantastic body, all muscle and hardness and the perfect mix of soft hair covering his pecs and trailing lower to the waist of his jeans.

She took another step closer, feeling a lot of things she'd never expected, all of them shame for doing the one thing she'd sworn she wouldn't. "I really didn't hear him, Jed. I would never just walk away." She stood in front of him, looking down on him, wishing he'd do something, anything, to make her feel better.

He rested his arm on his leg. "Diana, I know you wouldn't, but the fact is you did. You get so involved with what you're working on that you put everything else aside. It's just been the boys and me for so long, and having all of you is probably selfish of me, but they need you still. I need you, and you disappearing for days, burying yourself in whatever you're working on, isn't going to work. You really upset Danny, and Christopher needed you today. Everything was about you, from a bug he found that had these pretty colors he knew you would love, to a cut on his finger that only you could fix. He just wanted an excuse to see you. They love you so much that everything they see and do, they want to share with you. You're their mother. I'm here for so many things and do all I can, but you've always been their anchor, Diana."

"It doesn't sound like you got much done today." Diana was aware that Jed wasn't one for dramatics. He said it like it was, but he would have downplayed their distress and had most likely spent the entire day keeping the boys from her.

He shook his head. "Mom was here, and Dad. They helped, but it wasn't the same, Diana. They needed you. They're used to having you all the time. A few hours a day without you is fine, doable, even, but for two days you were here and completely unavailable to them. They're too young for that, and they don't understand the kind of drive you have. They shouldn't have to compete with that."

She just wanted to help this man. That was all she wanted to do.

"I'm tired," Jed said. "I'm going to have a shower and then go to bed." He dumped his shirt in the hamper and walked into the bathroom, then closed the door.

She listened to the shower turn on and felt a distance

in their room for the first time, remembering her mother being completely inaccessible to her. It was a thought that sickened her as she sat down on the bed. With her husband in the shower and her children down the hall, she was unable to fight her misery at the idea that she'd failed her family.

Chapter 13

"Diana, it will do your boys good to see you achieve, to succeed and be an amazing lawyer," Becky said. "Show them you can do it all, be their mother, a wife, and work." She was sitting in one of the deck chairs at the patio table with Diana as she finished her coffee, watching over the boys playing in the backyard on that sunny Sunday morning. Jed stood in the doorway, watching over his wife and how quiet she was.

She'd pulled into herself, he'd realized, and now he was starting to feel like crap, seeing her like this. Last night after he'd come out of the shower, she'd said nothing, having changed and climbed into bed, huddling into a ball. She'd only swiped at her face, unable to hide the tears she'd shed. This morning, she'd been hovering around the boys again, far from her cheerful self.

"Mom's right, Diana." He couldn't believe he'd said something so supportive, but stifling Diana was something he couldn't do, either. She loved what she did, but she also loved being a mother, and he didn't like to see her being forced to choose. She gave all of herself into whatever she did, and he could see how much he'd hurt her the night before.

She smiled stiffly but didn't quite look his way. Ouch!

"Doesn't matter, really," she said. "It was foolish of me to think I could do both. You should be happy that I'm not going to practice law, Jed." Maybe she didn't realize how it had come out, but it sounded as if there was some blame coming his way.

"Diana, knock it off. I never said to quit. That was all you this morning." He stayed where he was, leaning in the doorway. "I know you feel bad, Diana, but pulling out completely isn't the answer."

"Maybe so, Jed, but you can't tell me that didn't make you happy." She scooted around in her chair, setting her coffee down on the table. Her vibrant blue eyes, so conflicted moments ago, were now filled with fire.

"I'd be lying to you if I said that wasn't true, but I want you to want to be here, Diana. No one is happy if you're not, and I don't want you blaming me down the road because you can't be. This has to be your choice, Diana. Otherwise we're heading down a road I don't want to go down." He took in the boys, running and laughing, and Diana, who seemed beyond enjoying this simple moment. "Like right now, Diana. It's Sunday morning, and here you are, sitting upset and wrapped up in your guilt. You may be here right now, but you've checked out." He shook his head. "That's not good for the boys, for you, or for me, so make a decision on what you want, Diana, what's going to make you happy, and then we'll figure the rest out."

His mom stared out at the boys and then back at Jed. "Jed, why don't you go give your dad a hand with the luggage? See if he's ready to leave for the airport yet," she said. Having his mom here in the middle of this would have bothered him at any other time. That she had asked him to help his dad with a few bags that would already be loaded into the trunk of the car made Jed shake his head, but maybe his mom could be the voice of reason his wife needed right now, considering the only thing he wanted to do was shake some sense into her.

"Diana, he's gone now, so why don't you tell me what's really going on? I saw how excited you got when you started researching for Carl, trying to help him. I've seen it before, this little something that seems to come alive inside you every time you use your legal mind. Yet now you want to toss it away."

Didn't Becky get how she was feeling, coming down to a choice between being a lawyer and her boys? There wasn't one, there couldn't be. "My boys come first. My family has to," Diana said. She squeezed the handle of her mug, feeling her mother-in-law's hand touch her.

"Hey, who says you have to choose?"

She wanted to say Jed did, or he had, but the truth was that he'd herded the kids and handled everything at home so she could bury herself in work. The only person she could point fingers at was herself.

"Diana?" Becky prodded again, and this time, when Diana looked over to her, she was consumed with guilt.

"Me, it was me. It was hard hearing I was so wrapped up in someone else that I'd put my children second. That was what my mother always did. We were never her first or even second thought."

"You're not your mother, not even close to being

someone like her. Maybe going down there to that meeting wasn't such a good idea. I wondered after if I pushed you into doing something that maybe Jed was right about. It would've been best to leave that rock unturned. Sometimes it's best to leave things as they are."

"You're not to blame. No, I'm glad you encouraged me. Even though it was difficult to be there, to listen, I feel as if I can put that part of me, that part of my life, behind me for the first time. I guess I carried this ghost of the past around for so long I'd forgotten that it was over. Being there, seeing her again and listening to her talk about it, I didn't feel crippled emotionally. Sometimes confronting that ghost can put to rest all your worries. She can't hurt me anymore. She has no power over me." She hadn't even realized until she said it now. "She's my past, not a part of my future."

"Then why are you so quick to just close off a part of you that needs to help others? You're a good lawyer, Diana."

"How do you know that?" she said. It felt good having someone say so to her, even if she didn't think Becky was impartial.

"Because you're an amazing mother, and you never just do half of anything. You pour all of yourself into whatever task you're involved in. And before you cut your nose off to spite your face and decide to close the door on that sharp mind of yours, understand this: Life is a balance. You have to learn when to be a lawyer, a mom, and a wife. It's like from one to three, you're a lawyer, handling problems, doing what you do, and as soon as that clock hits three, you're not anymore. You're now a mom and a wife to Jed. Being a woman means greatness because you can do so much more once you learn how to switch hats. There will be times that something comes up. Maybe the boys are sick and you can't work, or you have to put a few more hours in."

She understood what Becky was saying, but her problem was being able to shut down the work side, because she'd always be in the middle of reading, drafting, or researching something important. "I think that's maybe my problem. I'm not ready to shut the door on my kids, and I'm afraid of trying again, of taking a case and getting so absorbed that I don't hear them. When Jed told me last night about how I brushed off Danny and the number of times they wanted to race over and tell me something, it broke my heart. I know when I start digging into the law and working, it takes all of me, and I want to cry thinking of my kids seeing me here but not being able to talk to me." Her throat thickened and ached, so she pulled a shaky breath.

"I understand that, Diana, I really do, and I'm pretty sure Jed does, as well. He loves you, and maybe you're not ready, but I'm going to remind you again: You are not your mother. Nor do you have any of her characteristics other than looking like her. I've got to tell you, you're a beautiful woman, but stop comparing yourself to Faye. Everything you see is on the surface, and there's nothing lovely or cute or even beautiful about just that."

She looked at her boys and Christopher, who was running her way, crying after falling and scraping his knee. "I know that. My mother never had empathy for anyone but herself."

Christopher was in her arms, burying his head against her as she kissed his cheek and took in the scrape on his knee, lifting his leg and kissing it better for him. Then he climbed down as if that simple touch had solved everything for him.

When she looked back up at Becky, she noticed Jed and Rodney coming around the side, chatting.

"Glad you see and understand that," Becky said. She reached out and touched Diana's hand, gave it a squeeze, and called out to Rodney that it was time to go home.

Chapter 14

"It was nice having your parents here again, your mom." Diana came up behind him as he watched his parents drive away, slipping her arms around his waist.

"Yeah, but with them goes the built-in babysitter," he said. He breathed easier having her hands on him again. Whatever his mother said had somehow brought down the wall of self-pity Diana had erected. "At least you feel better." He reached behind himself, sliding his arm around her shoulder, pulling her beside him and against him. Her hand slipped so easily to his chest. He kissed her forehead as she rested her head against his shoulder.

"I do. I mean, I still feel like crap, and I ache inside every time I think of my boys needing to tell me something when I wasn't available to them. I swore I'd never do that, be that way."

Now he couldn't help feeling bad for laying it on her last night. "They'll survive, Diana, and it was just because you were here and I asked them to leave you be. All those things they had to tell you, they won't even remember them, because they were just a ruse to be with their mom."

She was holding him tight, leaning against him, resting her chin on his chest, watching him. "That's the thing, Jed. Talking, sharing, just seeing that I'm here is important to them, to be able to tell me they're sad, or they found an amazing, disgusting bug, or to have their noses wiped or their lunches made, or to get a hug just because they need it. It's their way of saying they love me, and they need me to be here for them. Maybe I took that for granted, and hearing you tell me how they felt, being unavailable, helped me decide a lot of things. The fact is that no children should feel they can't talk to Mom or Dad."

"Diana, you're an amazing mom. Maybe I should have told you that, because I was being a little selfish, too, you know. I wanted to be able to bug you, too, to talk to you, and I couldn't, and it's not the fact you were working. It was more that you buried yourself for two days, doing exactly what I knew you would."

She rubbed her face against his chest and pulled away. "I don't know how to be half a lawyer. It's demanding, the work, and your mom already talked to me about putting aside time." She shrugged. "Maybe this isn't the right time. Maybe it needs to wait until the boys are older."

The phone was ringing, and Danny and Christopher were running around out front.

"I'll go get it." She stopped, looking out at the boys, and he could see the worry.

"They're fine, Diana. I'm here watching them."

What it really came down to was that his children were happy having all this open area to run and play in, with two parents here who loved them. It was a simple thing.

"Jed, I need to run into town and meet with Carl." Diana appeared in the doorway, holding the phone, pulling her lower lip between her teeth. "Can you watch the boys?"

He glanced out at them and the horses in pasture, grazing. "Yeah, I can, but this is Sunday, Diana, family time. Why don't you tell Carl to come here? If you're doing work from here, he can come to you." To make sure Carl understood he wouldn't have his wife running in circles, that her time was valuable, he'd be here man to man. He wasn't about to have anyone taking advantage of Diana's generosity. The time she was giving, she'd better be compensated for it.

He wondered for a second whether she was going to argue before she shrugged. "Fine," she said, then redialed the phone. At least one thing would come out of Jed being here: He'd make sure she didn't come out of the meeting with something else that would bury her for days and have them back at square one, with Diana feeling like crap and Jed feeling like he'd lost his wife.

Chapter 15

Why Jed was being so obstinate about her leaving the house now, she didn't know. She'd already told him she was done, packing in the fleeting thought of her brief career as a lawyer. She'd listened to her mother-in-law and understood what she had said, and to Jed, although she knew deep down he'd never wanted her to work. She had to be honest. The man wasn't going to let her put any of this on him, as he'd gone out of his way to step it up. This was all on her.

She pulled out her notes and her printed recommendations, feeling bad for billing Carl for the little she'd been able to do. She'd managed to contact a Vancouver lawyer willing to help him, and her notes had already been emailed. She stopped for a moment, seeing how she could lose herself, helping someone out. She sat down in the soft chair beside the desk, wondering how some women managed to pull it off. Then she glanced up to the wall, which had photos of her and Christopher after he was born, and another of Jed and her with the boys. Their family was so complete, her best achievement yet.

She heard voices, a woman, and it took only a second for her to realize it was her mother. There was a man, too, and she could hear Jed as well as they came down the hall. She hadn't heard a car door, and she also couldn't help wondering why her mother was there.

"Diana? Carl is here." Jed was in the doorway, and her mother was with Carl. Faye smiled at Diana, and for the life of her she couldn't figure out whether there was anything genuine there.

Maybe Jed understood her uncertainty, as he stepped in and said, "Carl, Diana will meet with you here. Faye can wait with me."

She nodded to her husband, realizing he could read her better than anyone. She loved him so much, and maybe he understood. His gaze met hers, and she sent her love to him as he smiled at her and then guided Faye away.

"Carl, glad you could come. I've done a lot of research and reading for you." She directed Carl, who was so tall, wearing a light collared shirt and khakis, to a chair she had placed in front of the desk. He was a nice-looking man.

"Thank you, Diana," Carl said as he sat.

She opened the file after scooting into her own chair and slid it across the table, her recommendations. "As you know, because of the situation, a Canadian lawyer will have to handle the application, but I've already taken the liberty of contacting one in Vancouver who specializes in—"

"Diana," Carl interrupted, gently placing his hand over hers where she was pointing to the first of the items on her outline.

She glanced up into soft brown eyes, a little bloodshot, but holding a sympathy she hadn't seen before.

"I can see the amount of work you've done, and I really appreciate it. When your mother insisted I contact you, that you would be simply the best lawyer who would do everything to help me, she was right. I had contacted another in town who'd already indicated that this wasn't his area of expertise."

She sat back, looking at Carl, wondering why her mother would have pushed so hard. What was her angle? The Faye she knew didn't have a maternal bone in her body, and everything was about what was good for herself.

"I can see you're a little surprised. Listen, Faye told me long ago about her past, your relationship. It's caused her a lot of pain, knowing she couldn't be a good mother. We all have regrets, Diana. I've got kids I haven't seen in so long because I was an awful parent. Do you know I took from my kids—all of them, just to be clear? I took their birthday money, emptied their piggy banks to feed my addiction."

Maybe it was the shock in her face that he gestured to. She was horrified, thinking of her own children and someone doing that.

"I was so desperate, and this was after I had taken out a second and third mortgage on the house, after I had forged my wife's signature. I was emptying pockets, cleaning out bank accounts, accounts started years ago by my ex-wife's parents for the kids, until there was nothing. My kids started coming and asking what had happened to all their money and why there was nothing in their plastic little banks. My wife, well, that was when she started to question what was going on, but I always had a line for everything, so casting doubt was easy. It must have been the cleaning lady before we let her go, or one of the kids' friends." He made a face and waved his hand. "It didn't matter. I was good at the lies rolling off my tongue just so I could keep on feeding that addiction, making that bet. Rolling pennies, coins, then stealing whatever I could until I hit rock bottom, stealing from the wrong person, who put an end to my downward spiral. That rock bottom got me this record. I lost my family, my home, my car. It was all gone."

She swallowed, looking at a man she hadn't known well, an acquaintance in town, realizing everyone had a story. She crossed her arms. Carl had bared everything to her. "And your ex-wife contacted you?" she said. She couldn't imagine ever reaching out to a husband who'd betrayed her.

He nodded. "It was my son's request. If it was up to Nelly, I'm sure she'd be happy strapping me to a stake and lighting the match. For the past few years, I've been writing, sending money, what I could, to try to make up for what I've done. I wasn't sure if they were reaching them or if they were even reading my letters. I was sending them to Nelly's parents. When Nelly called, told me about Seth…" He opened his hands, gesturing help-lessly. "I may have been the worst excuse for a parent, but, God willing, I was there when my son was born, and saying goodbye to my son, being able to say I'm sorry in person, to hold his hand as he leaves us…it's as if I'm being given a second chance. Do you understand?"

"I do." She did, to a point, not wanting to experience what Carl was going through. Maybe that was why she'd pushed so hard, giving everything to helping him and then ignoring her own children. She picked up a pen and was about to reach for the paper in front of Carl when he picked it up instead.

"Diana, I can see what you've done and will call this Vancouver lawyer. What I'm saying is that your mother is me. She's trying. She wants to make amends for what she's done." He held up his hand to her, and she could feel her back going up.

To her, it was different, what she'd lived through. He had to understand that much. "Carl, I appreciate what you're saying, and sharing what happened with your family, but too much happened between my mother and me—and my sister, who's no longer here."

He leaned back in his chair, nodding, watching her again with sympathy. "I'm just saying, Diana, that it's not good to hold on to the past. Let it go. It would be different if she were still up to her old tricks, but she's doing her best. We all slip up, but getting right back on that road, putting one foot in front of the other, is what we do." He gestured to himself, but she understood his meaning.

"I'm just saying, don't be so quick to close the door in her face," he said. "It took a lot of guts for her to come forward, to reach out to you and say she's sorry, and to keep coming back." He stood up and reached out across the desk. She shook his hand. It was warm and firm, confident. "Just remember something: It's easier to hate than it is to forgive." He took a step to the door. "Oh, and that husband of yours…good man, very protective."

She frowned for a moment. "Yes, he is."

Carl smiled over at her. "You'll send a bill to me for your time?"

She hadn't planned on it, considering she felt guilty for not being able to come through and resolve the situation for Carl herself.

"Diana, please send me a bill. It's the least I can do to make sure you're compensated. I wouldn't want your husband thinking I took advantage of you in any way. His warning already came through loud and clear."

"His warning? When was this? What did he say?"

He smiled warmly. "Oh, I had a feeling when we pulled in and Jed was waiting. He didn't have to say much after letting me see your boys, just mentioned that the work had taken you away from them and him, and if I had any ideas about you jumping through hoops for me, I needed to get them out of my head. Got to respect a man who protects what's his."

Then Carl left, and Diana wondered what else Jed had said that she didn't know about.

Chapter 16

"Well, it's so nice for us to have a moment together alone while Diana is in with Carl," Faye said, and Jed couldn't get over her resemblance to his wife.

That was where it ended, though, because personality wise, Faye and Diana were about as opposite as two could get. Faye was bubbly, outgoing, could focus all her attention on a man as if everything he said was the most important thing in the world. For a moment, he could see how some could get taken in by her charm.

They were outside on the deck, Faye taking a seat in one of the lounge chairs while the boys ran and played. She watched them after their quick greeting, the interest and the questions they'd tossed her way. The concept of being a grandmother to the boys was something she didn't seem to understand. With Becky having given them a firm foundation of a grandmother's role, he could tell the boys weren't quite getting the non-maternal concept of Faye. She didn't hug them or talk to them on their level, and she would be the last to get down with them on the floor and play. He wondered whether that was something she even knew how to do.

"You're very quiet, Jed. You have a nice family, and it does my heart good to know that Diana has a good man looking after her." She flashed him one of her million-dollar smiles again.

He didn't say anything, just watched her as he stretched out his legs in the other lounge chair he was sitting in, watching his boys. He could feel Faye fidgeting without looking her way. What was it about people who needed to fill the silence? "So what's the deal with you and Carl?" he said, watching the reaction in Faye's expression.

She firmed her lips. "Well, he's my friend, the first one I had in this town when I came back, the first who gave me a chance and didn't slam the door in my face. He's also the one who encouraged me to make the effort with Diana."

Really? So it was Carl he needed to pay a visit to, get him to back off from sticking his nose in, trying to reconnect Faye and Diana with some reconciliation that, in his book, wasn't going to happen.

"Why did you come back here, Faye? I mean, this isn't a place that could have any good memories for you after how you left."

Her smile faded, and he noticed a mix of unreadable emotions on her face. "No, there are no good memories, although at the time it felt as if this place was all I had. I found out Diana was here, and I was surprised, if truth be told." She started to laugh as if any of this was funny, and maybe it was Jed's expression that made her realize he wasn't impressed by what she was saying.

"Look, it bothers me a lot, all of it," she said. "Coming back here after what happened with Todd and his son, losing everything and then learning my baby had married a Friessen…" She gestured toward him. "People talk. It wasn't too hard to find out where she was, and all. Heard Andy moved away, too, has some young wife and a pile of kids. It was all people could talk about, how Andy had walked away from his family for this girl, a maid. She must have been something."

He didn't know what to make of Faye. "She's a wonderful young woman, Laura. She's family. Andy's family."

"He did all his daddy's dirty work, you know. He was always the enforcer, and his daddy…"

Jed wasn't sure he wanted to go down this line of questioning with Faye. He said nothing in answer to her prompting. He didn't like when people trawled, and it seemed that quality had been bred into Faye.

She laughed and gestured. "Okay, I'm just going to ask, then. Todd, how is he? What's he been up to?"

Was she kidding? He sighed. "What exactly is it you're after, Faye? Todd Friessen is a dog, and if you're here because you're looking to hook back into his scene or him…and you somehow have this idea that Diana is your ticket—"

"Excuse me, sir!" she snapped. "I wouldn't think to drag my daughter back into that side of the Friessens. It's done my heart proud to see she's doing well. She made something of herself. You seem like a good man who's looking after my daughter, giving her stability, respectability, so she can hold her head high and have what she deserves to have. As for Todd, I'm not looking for any of that back, but when someone has affected you and been so much a part of who you were in such a horrible way, it's just…" She shrugged as if she couldn't finish.

"Uncle Todd will go on his way, as he always has. He's loyal to no one but himself. Andy isn't cut from the same cloth. So, honestly, are you looking to seek Todd out and start something up with him?"

He could hear footsteps, and he looked up to see Carl standing in the doorway, watching them.

"Well, are you, Faye?" Carl asked, and Faye looked up as if she'd been caught doing something she shouldn't.

Chapter 17

He waited until Diana had gone to bed and said nothing to her about Faye. Even after Carl had asked Faye about her intentions—and he wondered now whether she even understood her own mind—he had driven them away in his older Buick, the tension between the two ramped up from the unanswered question. Everyone knew what a dog Todd Friessen was.

Jed had said nothing to Diana, not wanting to drag her into the nightmare of her past. If Faye was all about searching out Todd Friessen—and for what purpose?—he didn't want Diana knowing anything about it. Right now, he was certain of only one thing: Faye herself didn't seem to understand whether she was here to extract something she thought she was owed or whether she was so hooked on Todd Friessen that she thought she could rekindle something with him, a man who went through women as if each were yesterday's news. From what he'd known of how bad it had gone down with Faye, Andy, and Todd, with the fact that drugs had been involved and Faye had done something equally bad just to get back at his uncle, he felt their reunion could blow up on everyone—namely, his wife.

He dialed the phone and listened to it ring, standing in the kitchen. If Diana was still awake, she wouldn't be able to hear him.

"Hello?" Neil sounded distracted.

"Didn't catch you at a bad time, did I?"

"Hey, Jed, how's things? No, not bad, just trying to figure things out, is all." He sighed on the other end.

Jed couldn't help wondering where Neil was with trying to figure out the next move for him and his wife, starting over in that small coastal community near Brad. "How're Candy and the kids?"

"Fantastic! Michael is walking and into everything, and Candy has me baby proofing cabinets and drawers. Cat adores her baby brother, and she's been practicing her words and talking by reading the early readers to him. Never seen Candy so happy here, too."

He could almost hear the smile in his brother's voice when he spoke of Candy and the kids. He was glad, since Neil had almost screwed up everything because of his need to have it all.

"So what's up?" Neil asked, always getting straight to the point.

"Diana's mother. Don't know if you've talked with Mom and Dad?"

"Not since they left here. What's going on with Faye? She didn't show up again, did she?"

He wondered now whether it had been such a good idea, him phoning Neil and involving him. "She's been back a few times. Diana just didn't tell me, and Mom was here and went with Diana to some addictions meeting Faye is part of. It's a long story, but I'm not sure what her intentions are, and I don't want her messing with Diana. Diana's vulnerable there, and her mom plays up a pretty good story of trying to make amends."

"What has Faye said she wants?"

"That's the thing. She dances around it, but this last time she brought up Andy and Todd and her curiosity about the Friessens and what Uncle Todd is up to. I just can't help feeling she's either got some unreconciled issues, an agenda, or something else, and it's that something else that I'm afraid of. I don't want Diana getting caught up in it."

"You think she's trying for money?" Neil said.

It was the first thing Jed had thought, even when she'd laid the flirting on a little thick with him. She had to know he was immune to that sort of thing. He had eyes only for his wife.

"I don't know. I would've thought that if that was what she was after, she'd have worked on Diana, but so far…I don't know, Neil, but when she brought up Todd in her next breath, I knew it wasn't just to make conversation. I don't know, but it's—"

"She won't leave Diana alone is what you're saying. I saw how messed up Diana was in Cancun. We love her, and she's your wife, but she's also our family, my sister-in-law. We made a promise to Diana when Mom called that family meeting. We all stand together, you know."

He could hear tapping in the background.

"Okay, just sent an email to Andy and Brad," Neil said.

"Hey, whoa, about what?"

"Time for the Friessen boys to come together, have a talk with Faye and send her on her way." Neil was sounding as if this was just a piece of business he needed to take care of.

"A little presumptuous, don't you think, Neil? After all, Diana's my wife. I just can't help thinking that if Faye's here about Todd, this could end up backfiring and dragging Diana into something that has nothing to do with her."

"That's why…oh, hey, look! Andy must have been online. He's already answered. He's going to come back, meet us at your place."

Jed held the phone away from his ear, staring at it. "Neil, I didn't call you to wrangle the troops."

"Look, Jed, maybe I'm overstepping, but we made a promise to be there, so let's meet, track Faye down, all of us, and put an end to this so Diana can have some peace and you don't have to worry Faye's going to be sneaking in the back door."

Maybe Neil was right.

"If I remember, not too long ago, it was all of you who were standing there with me," Neil said, "and if I've learned one thing, Jed, it's that we're a family. Although we could solve things alone, it's better together, letting people know it isn't just one of us they're messing with. They get all of us."

After Jed said goodbye, he held the disconnected phone, wondering what he'd been thinking. When he set it back in its cradle, he realized Neil was right. Between him, Neil, Brad, and Andy, they should be able to find exactly what Faye Claremont's intentions were in coming back to North Lakewood. And God help her if she had any intention of dragging Diana back into her world.

Chapter 18

She was having the most erotic dream. Jed was inside her, pulling in and out. The sensations were exquisite, and she found herself moaning as a hand skimmed down over her bare skin, her stomach and thighs. She wanted to complain when she was rolled onto her back, her arms tied with a scarf to the bedframe so she couldn't reach for Jed. He pressed kisses down her neck and around her breasts, over her stomach and lower, and she hissed and arched up, realizing she was naked when she'd gone to bed in one of her nightgowns. She blinked then, realizing the bathroom light was on, casting a soft shadow over her husband, who seemed determined to pleasure her until she was begging and screaming for more. He hooked her legs over his shoulders and held her with his hands.

"Jed," she cried out, but he didn't seem of the mind to hear her or listen or stop. It was as if he was going to take her to the brink of madness and have her screaming and begging, and he still wouldn't stop. She couldn't recognize her voice or the words as she pulled at the bindings that held her hands and then tossed her head side to side.

Before she could come back down from the haze, he pushed a pillow under her butt, holding her wide as he entered her, and she gazed up into the heat in his expression and the desire he had for her as he moved again, harder, holding her as he pushed deeper and stilled, slowing his pace as if making each movement count, painfully slow. When she closed her eyes and gasped, he withdrew, and she wanted to cry at the loss.

"Look at me, Diana. I want you to see me as I come apart inside you and know that it's me who's here with you, your husband. I want this moment now. Look at me!"

Her eyes flew open, and Jed held her legs so she couldn't move and slammed into her again, pushing the breath out of her with each movement, hard, deep, over and over until she could see he couldn't hold back, and it was at that moment, when she was going to break apart, that he leaned over her, slamming into her again, allowing his seed to spill warm inside her.

Her legs started to shake from being spread for so long and having him still buried inside her. She also wasn't sure she could trust her voice to speak again when Jed reached forward and untied her hands.

Then he pulled out, rolling to the side and taking her with him.

"Wow, that was some way to wake me up." She licked her lips, pressing a kiss to his chest.

He grunted, his hand saying a different story as his fingers caressed her side as if he couldn't get enough of touching her. She skimmed her foot over his leg, over the front to his foot.

"You're trying to get me pregnant again, aren't you?"

she said. She knew he was, considering the number of times, as of late, that he'd taken her by surprise when the boys weren't around. At night, he'd been waking her more and more as he slid inside her.

He pressed a kiss to her forehead. "And if I am?" he teased her, and she rolled, resting her crossed arms on his chest, looking up at the grin on his face.

"We have two very active boys, and we have time for more?" she said. Then again, she'd just packed away her law career for some time down the road when she wasn't as busy, so her boys wouldn't have to compete for her time.

"Honestly, Diana, now is when I want them, while they're young, close in age. I saw you holding Sarah. You want one even though you wanted to practice law, too. This is a time we should be having our kids. I expected you to tell me you wanted another, and I had it in my head that I was going to have fun giving you one, but when you didn't, I'd already convinced myself it was going to happen. If they're closer in age, not as spread out, they'll be in school at the same time, and you'll have time to work."

"So you're really saying you'd be okay with me working again?"

"Someday, yes, when you can balance both, but let's have our kids now, more," he said, and she was stuck on the "more" part, wondering just how many he was talking about.

He reached down and tucked her hair behind her ears. "You're my wife, Diana. I want a houseful of kids with you."

"And if we don't have any more?" She needed to know if this was something that would eventually come between them.

The way he watched her, she wondered for a moment whether he'd misunderstood. "Tell me, is that what you want, Diana? If me getting you pregnant again isn't what you want…"

"Jed," she said, stopping him, rubbing her hand over the light hair on his chest. "I never said that. I love our boys, and I would love another. I'm just saying, are you okay if it doesn't happen?"

"Diana, I have everything I need here with you and the boys. Let's just see what's in the cards for us, okay?"

The way he looked at her, the love he had for her, Diana knew that even if they didn't have any more kids, they were going to be okay.

Chapter 19

J ed was still in the shower after pulling her in with him. He'd gotten home from taking the boys to kindergarten and preschool but had let her sleep after waking her up in the middle of the night to make love to her. She should be sore after the last time, the way he'd held her against the shower wall and drove into her again and again, but she could feel part of him inside her now, and it made her feel complete and whole, so compliant that she would do anything for him.

She was still smiling when she heard a car coming, and she walked to the window, doing a double take as she noticed a light SUV. She was in her housecoat and was about to go and put some clothes on when she recognized Brad driving, with Neil in the passenger side. What the hell were Jed's brothers doing here? Then they saw her, and Neil stepped out and waved, so she was stuck. She pushed open the screen door and stepped outside, knowing how she looked, her hair still wet.

The back door opened, and Andy stepped out, all of them dressed, as they always were, in dark blue jeans.

Brad wore a dark blue long-sleeved shirt, Andy a salmon-colored T-shirt and dark glasses, and Neil, always the most nicely dressed of all of them, wore a dark green dress shirt. He pulled off his shades and tucked them into its front. "Did we wake you? It's almost lunch time," he teased as he started up the steps.

Diana pulled at the front of her housecoat, holding it at the neck, feeling her face warm as Neil hugged her and kissed her cheek. "So what are you doing here? Not that I'm not glad to see you." She glanced down at Andy, who was standing on the bottom steps, looking up at her. Brad gave her shoulder a squeeze, leaned down, and kissed her cheek.

They all seemed to be looking at each other, maybe deciding on what to say. "I take it Jed didn't tell you we were coming," Brad said, watching her in that big-brotherly way he did.

"Did something happen with the estate, Andy?" she said, hoping he wasn't getting dragged back into that cesspool. His mother was still messing with him from beyond the grave.

"I called them," Jed said from behind her as he pushed open the screen door. She hadn't heard him coming. "Can't believe you're already here. What did you do, drive right out?

"Figured the sooner, the better. We grabbed Andy from the airport. He took an early flight," Neil said.

Diana was really confused as she glanced to Jed and down to Andy, who was watching her through dark glasses. She couldn't figure out for the life of her what this was about.

"We heard your mother's been back here again," Neil said.

She turned to Jed, feeling betrayed. "Excuse me,

what are you doing? You called your brothers because… what? What are you planning to do? She's been here. Who knows what she's doing?" She gestured at them all. "Does it matter anymore?"

She wasn't going to fall apart like she had the first time her mother had shown up, and she had gone to the meeting as her mother had wanted. The woman was more interested in her helping Carl than anything else, and she wasn't too interested in delving deeply into their relationship. She was ready to let all of that go. She'd done what she could to help the man, and now she was moving on.

"It does matter, Diana, especially since your mom may have some hidden agenda where Todd Friessen is concerned," Jed said.

She couldn't have been more shocked. Her face heated, and she felt her heart skip a beat. "What does her being back have anything to do with Todd Friessen?"

"Apparently your mother has some unresolved interest in my dad," Andy said, "and we're all concerned about what that could mean, especially since Faye has always been a chameleon. We're worried that whatever she does could end up coming back on you." He pulled off his sunglasses, and his dark brown eyes were filled with something dark and dangerous—not toward her but on her behalf.

"Where are all of you getting this from? Faye has never said one thing about Todd Friessen."

Jed's hand was on her shoulder, turning her around, sliding down her back. "Outside with me, when you were speaking with Carl, she asked about him. When I tried to find out what her game was, she shut down. She told me a lot of things, like that she hasn't figured out what it is she's doing or wants. Maybe she's got some sick, twisted plan that could include dragging you back into something you have no business being part of."

As Diana looked from Jed, to Brad, to Neil, and then to Andy, she realized that however history was replaying, she was no longer a little girl fighting a bunch of bullies trying to hurt her mother and casting her into the same lot. She now had an army of Friessens, her fairytale knights, all fighting her battle as if it were their own.

"Okay," she said. "So what happens first?"

Chapter 20

"You didn't think you could give me a call letting me know you were on your way?" Jed said, watching as Diana slipped away to get dressed. Neil was in the kitchen, grabbing coffee.

"I thought Neil had," Brad said, glancing to Andy, who shrugged and pulled out his cell phone, which must have buzzed, as he turned his back to take the call.

"I expected Diana to be a lot more upset. She seems to be handling the issues with her mother better. Are you sure Faye is here to cause trouble? I know what Neil said had me and Andy rounded up and ready to get out here."

"That was my dad," Andy said, pocketing his phone and standing shoulder to shoulder with Brad, glancing to the door. "He hasn't heard from Faye."

"Is he still in town?" Brad asked.

"Who?" Neil appeared in the doorway, holding a mug of steaming coffee. He still hadn't shaved off the beard he'd started.

"Todd. He's still at the estate," Andy said. "He's

surprised she's back, though. He said he hadn't heard she was in town, but then, Dad doesn't spend much time here anymore."

"So what's the plan?" Brad asked. "I presume first we go find her and talk to her."

"This comes down to her leaving my wife the hell alone. Whatever her reason for coming back here, she's not having a relationship with Diana. She's not using her name or benefiting from their connection in any capacity. She's not dragging my wife into any of her shenanigans."

"So what is it you're planning, Jed? I'd really like to know," Diana said, now dressed in blue jeans and a blue flowered shirt. She had a healthy glow, and her damp hair was pulled up.

"Well, for one, your mother has a way of dancing around things and sneaking in behind my back. When I tell her to stay away and then learn she's been coming back around anyway, refusing to listen to me…you can't trust someone like that, Diana." He was watching his wife standing there, her arms crossed. Brad lingered behind, leaning on the railing beside Neil, who was appearing a little too laid back, in Jed's mind.

"There's no reason for her to come back, Jed," Diana said. "She has what she wants. I helped Carl, so we're done. I really think you may be making more out of this than necessary. I really don't think she's the issue you're making her out to be."

"I remember a lot things, maybe better than you, Diana, about Faye," Andy said. He didn't step closer but was also watching Diana for her reaction. "Your mother's interest was just in herself. It wasn't you girls. I remember seeing the scrawny things you were—you having to care for a girl that was far from right, tiptoeing around Faye's many moods. Todd even mentioned it a time or two in passing, implying you'd never amount to much with Faye as your role model. To him it was a joke, but now, remembering it makes me ill. You think your mother's changed?"

Diana held her tongue.

"Just as I thought," Andy said. "You're terrified of being dragged back into whatever scheme or con or whatever it is that will ultimately blow up in her face. Diana, I'm pretty good at reading people. I'm sure you being this close, the wounds still raw, you couldn't say for sure one way or the other."

"No, Andy is right," Neil said from beside Brad. "Let's find out where Faye is and go talk with her."

"Jed, do you know where she's staying?" Brad asked.

"Whoa, wait a second," Diana said. "I think if you're going to track down my mother and pay her a visit, it should be with me there as well."

At any other time, Jed would have said no, but he knew Diana needed to be the one to close the door. He gestured toward her. "Fine, you're right."

He watched Diana go into the house, and Brad said, "You really think that's a good idea, letting Diana tag along?"

Jed watched the door and then looked at Andy, Brad, and Neil. He nodded. "I do. More than anything, Diana needs to know that where her mother is concerned, she'll never be alone again."

Chapter 21

They were piled into Neil's light SUV, Diana wedged in the middle seat in back between Andy and Jed. This time, Neil was driving, and there was something about driving headlong into her problem with these men, her family. They considered this their problem, as well, and she was the passenger along for the ride.

"No threats," Diana said, curious as to what they were going to do.

"Diana, we don't threaten. We help those who are lost find the right way when they can't find it themselves," Neil said, staring in the rearview mirror at her. He had his dark glasses on, and he was beginning to look like some notorious bad boy on a wanted poster.

"Pull in here," Jed said.

"The steak place? Haven't been here in years. Was always good. Can't believe they hired Faye to work here," Andy said.

"Carl did. Remember him?" Jed said, talking over Diana's head, his arm resting around her shoulders.

"The manager. Yeah, I do. You said Diana did some work for him?"

"Jed, I can't talk about any work I do for clients," Diana said as Neil parked. "Ever heard of privilege?"

"Point very well made, Diana," Neil said. "Your wife is going to be one hell of a lawyer. I may just have a job for her once I figure out what it is I'm going to do."

Jed made a rude noise. "Like hell," he said, then opened his door.

Brad, Jed, and Andy climbed out. Jed held his hand out, and Diana slipped hers into it. He didn't let go as they followed Brad, Neil, and Andy inside the restaurant. It was dark inside, and it took her a minute to realize that Andy had started speaking with Carl. She couldn't make it out, but next she knew, she was being herded into the closed restaurant to a round table in the center.

Jed was holding her chair, and she sat down and listened to the polite exchange.

"I'll go get Faye. She's in back." Carl paused and glanced down at Diana. "Thank you for all you did. That lawyer you put in touch with me sounded hopeful and expects to have everything tidied up so I can be up to see my son at the end of the week."

"That's such great news, Carl," Diana said. She was happy he would be able to at least have some closure with his son, no matter what happened.

Faye appeared in a white blouse and black pencil skirt, her long red hair hanging loose. Her eyes widened as she took in the Friessen men. "Well, Andy Friessen, I would recognize you anywhere. You're a little older, but you look the same." She looked at each of them, and Diana waited for Neil and Brad as they introduced themselves. "Well, I'm quite honored. Four handsome Friessen men here to see me with my daughter. Diana, you've done well. So what can I do for you here? Carl said you wanted to speak with me." She was still standing behind the empty chair.

"Sit down," Diana said, gesturing toward it. "It's my husband and family who want to talk with you.

Brad stood up and pulled the chair out while Faye sat. She smiled brightly, and Diana wondered for a minute whether she'd batted her lashes. She couldn't help being horrified.

"Relax," Andy whispered in her ear. She looked his way. "Your face said it all." He was speaking low enough that she doubted anyone else could hear.

"I'm sitting," Faye said. "Now, I have to ask again, is there a reason you're all here?"

"Why exactly did you really come back here, Faye?" Andy asked.

"Do you think you can burn me out again?" She sounded hurt and vindictive. No one said anything. "I'm sorry. I came back because this is where Diana is. She's my daughter. After everything that happened, I needed to come and patch things up with her. I have grandchildren now, and I'd like to have a relationship in whatever way I can that will work for you, baby." Faye turned all her attention on Diana. Jed's hand went over hers, which was clutching her jeans. He rubbed her hand until it relaxed.

"That sounds reasonable, Faye," he said, "but I was clear with you after the first time you showed up that you weren't welcome. I asked you not to come back, yet you did after—"

"You mean when you tried to strong arm me?" Faye said. "If there's one thing I know, it's how to get down and fight in the gutter. No one is going to tell me to steer clear of what's mine. Diana is my daughter." Faye leaned forward as if she wasn't afraid of anything they were going to do to her.

This was the first time Diana could remember her mother sounding confident, important.

"Diana's our family," Neil said. "You see us here. You may have given birth to her, but all of us—Andy, Brad, Jed—we're family, and family walks through fire for each other, so we're here to make sure you don't hurt her. When you're told to steer clear and you don't, you're messing with all of us."

"I guess I'd like to know why I'm so important now when I was never before?" Diana said.

"I regret all of that, I truly do, but you have to know after all these years that people can change. I've changed. I'm not that lost soul anymore."

"Aren't you, Faye? The lost one looking to score or scam?"

Diana's heart thudded when she heard the voice behind her. Everyone looked back, but her mother's face said it all.

"Todd, I…" She pressed her hand to her chest and just looked up at him.

Diana was shaking and squeezing Jed's hand as she glanced around at Todd, but this time when he looked at her and then Andy beside her, she couldn't make sense of what he was thinking, whether he was about to cast her in with her mother or not.

"Could you excuse us? Faye," he said, gesturing for her to follow him. Diana just watched as Faye crossed the room with Todd out of earshot.

"Why's your father here?" Diana spun around in her seat to Andy, fighting the panic to jump up.

"Supposed to find out what score, if any, your mother has to settle with him. If we're right and this entire situation of Faye showing up for you was all about Todd, then I'd say this is his mess and he needs to clean it up."

Diana just stared at Andy when she finally understood what he was saying. He was here for her just like Brad and Neil. Whatever cleanup Andy had done for Todd years before, he was never going to do it again.

Chapter 22

The phone was ringing as soon as Diana got home from picking up her boys. She raced inside and grabbed it. "Hello?" She could see out the back window, where Brad, Neil, Andy, and Jed were building a fire in the pit, with chairs around it. They had talked about roasting some marshmallows later for the boys, and Jed would grill burgers and dogs on the barbecue for dinner.

"Diana, it's your mother, Faye."

She wanted to roll her eyes, as if she needed reminding who Faye was. "Faye, what can I do for you?"

"I wanted to say goodbye," she said.

"You're leaving?" Well, it was a good thing. She should be happy. The problem was that after today, she had realized that anything about her mother, being here or leaving, all of it just made her sad.

"It's time. If anything, today, I was envious of the husband you have and the family you married into. I never imagined that kind of support existed, but those men circled you in a way I haven't seen before. I didn't come back to hurt you. I did a lot of bad things, but having you wasn't one of them."

Diana didn't know what to say. She watched her boys race over to their father and then run in circles, chasing their uncle Neil, who pretended they had to catch him.

"Are you still there?" Faye asked.

"Yes, I'm just watching my boys in the backyard, playing with their uncles, laughing, running. I've given that to them. I may not have had the kind of carefree childhood that every child should have, but my boys will."

"I wasn't a very good mother, Diana, but I hope one day you'll understand I'm not all bad. No matter what you think, in my way, I do love you."

She hadn't expected that. Her mother had always made her feel as if she was the reason she had nothing, as if it had been her fault. She cleared her throat. "So what happened today with Todd? I mean, after you spoke with him, you left."

"I would've thought your husband would tell you, or at least Todd. Can't believe you're part of his family now."

Who, Todd's? Was she serious? "Todd may be my husband's uncle, but we're not family."

"But Andy is, I see. I was quite surprised to see him and the support he had for you. He never offered that when you could've used it."

Diana stared at the phone again. There was a lot of blame to go around, but Faye was her mother and should've been the one who protected her. She'd failed. "You haven't answered me. What happened with Todd?"

"He's changed, not the same man I knew. All my anger I held on to for what he did to me, hurting me… he's nothing but an old man now. I guess he knew how hurt I was after what he did, tossing me away." Faye didn't say anything else. Maybe it had just been about Todd all this time.

"So where will you go?"

"Away, someplace where no one knows me, someplace I can start over, a fresh start. Carl is going to join me after he gets back from seeing his son." She laughed, but Diana realized that was her way of making light of a tense situation. "Carl is a good man. He's not Todd Friessen. Just had to convince him of that." Faye sighed again. "So goodbye, baby," Faye said, then hung up before Diana could say a word.

She set the phone in the cradle and paused at the window for a moment before stepping out the door to her husband and family.

Chapter 23

It was dark outside, and the boys were in bed when Jed saw Diana step out the back door. The fire crackled, and the stars were bright. "Faye left," he told his brothers. "I still can't believe she called Diana and said goodbye."

"Well, it was a short trip, which Em will be thankful for, but I know she was worried about Diana," Brad said.

"Candy, too. She was all over me to get out here and make sure Diana was okay. I think she was ready to come, herself," Neil added from where he sat in the plastic chair, his feet up on a log he would later toss in the fire.

"Laura's been helping our neighbor Kim with her wedding," Andy said, "but she also told me I'd better make sure nothing upsets Diana."

"How are Laura and the kids doing?" Jed asked just as Diana reached him, touched his arm, and sat on his lap. His arms went around her, holding her to him. She kissed him on the cheek.

"She's fantastic." Andy was all smiles. Jed had never

seen him so head over heels for a woman in his life. "The kids are a handful, and when they're tucked in bed at night, they look like angels—until they wake up, that is. Then Laura's on them for everything. I've never been happier, where we are and what we have." Andy took another swallow from the can of beer he was holding.

"How're you doing there, Diana?" Neil asked from across the fire.

Diana had already wrapped her arms around Jed's neck. "Good. A little shocked still, I think. I don't quite understand how Faye was convinced to leave. What did your dad say to her, Andy, do you know?"

"He asked her if she thought coming back here was a way to get back at him or rekindle something. Apparently she said it was neither. He didn't believe her, said that after what he'd done to her and all the bad things she'd done to herself, she couldn't be okay with him," Andy said.

"Well, how could she be?" Diana replied, looking at him.

Andy didn't say anything as he looked back. "No, I guess not. I know that Dad apologized to her, though."

"So it was an apology she was after," Brad said, shaking his head.

"Dad offered her money to go away," Andy said, and Jed could feel the moment Diana tensed. "But she turned him down."

Everyone stared at Andy as if he'd grown a third eye. After all this and the visits here to Diana, could Faye in fact only have been looking to make amends, to hear the words "I'm sorry"?

Diana let out a breath that had everyone turning to her. "I'm relieved, seriously. When your dad showed up and the words they had, I thought for sure something was going down, something bad. When she phoned to say goodbye, the timing was too curious. The old Faye would have taken the money, Andy. Maybe she has changed, or is trying to."

Jed took in the exchange with Neil and Brad and Andy. They didn't need to say anything for him to know they were all on the same page. "I hope so, too, Diana, but I'm glad she's doing it somewhere else. Sometimes a fresh start is the best thing."

Diana rested her head on Jed's shoulder, his arm around her, holding her in his lap. "Yeah, you're right," she said. "I'm lucky that I have far more than Faye will ever have—because I have you and the promise you made to me."

Diana lifted her head, gazing down at him. He knew the promise she meant, the vow he had made to love her forever.

Chapter 24
THE VISITOR

There was a tapping on the door. Diana could hear it distantly on some level as she lay almost comatose under the covers with the warmth of her husband curled around her. She didn't want to move as she felt Jed stir beside her.

"Seriously, someone had better have a good excuse, pounding on the door at this hour," Jed muttered. He sounded mad and tired, and Diana mourned his loss as he slid out from under the covers, taking the warmth she loved to snuggle against with him. She didn't want to open her eyes and peek at the clock to find out how early it was, but she did anyway, groaning as she read the digital readout: 6:09 a.m. Unbelievable!

The knocking started again, and she heard other mumbling—maybe Brad or Neil, she wasn't sure, as they had all stayed up pretty late around the fire, talking, chatting, and just catching up. Maybe it was someone lost or in trouble, and that thought made her sit up and reach for her housecoat. She pulled it on over her nakedness, and she could hear Jed talking to someone. He didn't sound happy. As she stepped into the hall, she bumped into Brad as he came out of Danny's room, where he'd been bunking down. He was pulling on his shirt, having already pulled on his jeans. Danny was sharing a bed with Christopher.

"You're awake, too?" Diana said, stifling a yawn.

"You usually have people dropping by at this hour?" Brad said. "Needed to get up anyway. Should be on the road early and getting back to Em."

They walked into the lights blazing in the front room, which revealed the open front door where Neil stood with Jed.

"This is ridiculous, Faye, coming here at this hour!" Jed sounded really mad. She didn't need to ask who was at the door.

"Look, I just need a minute with my daughter. This is really important." Faye sounded quite upset, and Diana couldn't help the childhood fear that came out of nowhere, warning her that Faye had done something yet again and was about to turn her home, where her children were asleep, upside down.

Diana was holding her arm across her stomach, her other hand snaking up to her throat, when Brad stepped around her to the door. He glanced at her, his gaze softening to understanding.

"Who's here?" she heard Andy ask from behind her, and she turned to see him rubbing his head, tired like the rest of them. He'd pulled on his clothes, his T-shirt hanging over his jeans, and she just stared at him.

"Faye," she whispered, and she swallowed, not knowing what else to say. She couldn't make out what Jed said before Neil spoke up, as well.

Diana couldn't take any more. "You know what? Stop this right now. You're going to wake the boys. Jed, just let her in so she can say what she came to say and then be gone." Diana didn't miss Andy shaking his head as he leaned against a chair back. Faye stepped in past an angry Jed.

"Whatever it is you need to say to Diana, you say it here with all of us," Jed said—not that Diana was interested in being alone with Faye. She was, in fact, grateful that Brad, Neil, and Andy were still here with her and Jed.

Faye did appear determined as she stepped inside. She had blue jeans on, and she pulled at her dark coat. Her hair hung loose, and she wore a light smattering of makeup. She appeared neatly put together as she looked at each of the men before letting her gaze fall on Diana. "Well, that was some greeting," she said, and Diana wanted to roll her eyes at her mother's dramatics.

"Why are you knocking on my door at six in the morning, getting us out of bed?" she said. Then again, when she was growing up, that was what Faye had done. Maybe nothing had changed.

"I was leaving, packed up, and was in my car, but I couldn't go yet because there was something I hadn't told you. I hadn't planned on saying anything at all, ever. It didn't seem as if I should until I saw you, Andy, with my daughter yesterday, side by side, as if this was another universe."

Diana sighed again. Faye was rambling, and she was tired and didn't want to get tied up in any games. Maybe Jed knew, as he stepped to her side, pulling her against him.

"Seriously, Faye?" he said.

Andy was just staring at her. Brad appeared confused, exchanging an odd look with Neil.

"Okay, look." Faye held both her hands in the air to

stop them as if she were upset. "This isn't about me, it was never about me, but when she paid me a visit about a month ago, I thought it was unusual. She scared me, that woman, she always did, but this isn't about me." Faye sounded nervous outside of the dramatics, and Diana was now wondering which "she" Faye was referring to.

"You're talking in circles. Would you get to the point?" Diana was a little surprised by how strong she sounded.

"I'm trying to, if you would just let me. This isn't helping me, stopping here and saying anything—quite the opposite. It would be best for me to just mind my own business, as I told her, and just be on my way, get on with my life and forget all about that little incident. But I couldn't."

"Faye, really, although I love a great mystery, at this hour I think I'll pass on the entertainment." Neil stepped closer, looking down on her. "Hurry up and spit it out."

Diana wondered, by the way Faye took in the badass look Neil had going on, whether she was going to flash him one of her million-dollar smiles and turn on the charm. *Please, no!*

"Okay, Mr. Hotshot, got all kinds of money and no time. I was just getting to that, and it's no skin off my nose if I say nothing. It's not as if you've done me no favors, so why, I have to ask myself, should I bother doing anything for all of you here? Well, I'm only here because of my daughter. That's the only reason I'm here at all—"

"Faye," they all said.

"It was your mother, Andy Friessen. Caroline. She paid me a visit."

Diana had to look at Andy, as they all did, and back

to Faye. "I don't understand why Caroline would pay you a visit. What exactly did she want?"

"Why, my dear, she wanted to know about you and how close you were to Andy's young wife, what your role was to her."

She didn't need to look Andy's way to know how still he'd gone.

"Are you telling me that Caroline Friessen paid you a visit asking about Laura?" Jed was holding Diana a little tighter.

"And about my daughter. She wanted to know about both of them." Faye turned and faced Andy then. "Andy Friessen, I'd just as soon not have said anything to you, but I have a conscience, and seeing you standing by my daughter now is the only reason I'm here to tell you your mother was fishing. I've seen it before. She was looking for dirt, and I don't know what it was, but I came only to warn you—and you." She turned to Diana then. "Even though I know she died not long after she appeared at the restaurant, she was looking for things, and that struck me as odd. Andy Friessen, your wife is a target, and my daughter may have become one by association."

Then Faye stepped forward and touched Diana's shoulder. "Okay, take care, baby. I'm off for good this time. I'm sure all of you will be sure to look after my daughter."

"Wait," Andy said.

Faye stopped in the doorway, and Diana was still trying to get her head around the fact that Andy's mother had paid Faye a visit.

"What did you say to her?" Andy asked, his voice laced with disbelief that Diana recognized.

Faye turned and faced Andy, staring at him as if she held all the cards. "Nothing at all. Told her I didn't know your wife, which I don't. Told her she could stick me in the ground and toss dirt over me before I'd ever speak to her of my daughter."

Then Faye walked out the door, and Diana was struck by something that passed between the brothers and Andy, as if they knew something she didn't.

"Okay," she said. "Does someone want to fill me in?"

Chapter 25

Diana was in the kitchen, making coffee. Neil had somehow convinced her that before they could discuss anything, they all needed a shot of caffeine.

"What do you think your mother was after?" Jed couldn't help asking Andy, who appeared a little shell shocked.

Andy rubbed his hand over hair tousled by sleep. "One of the things I was worried about, but why should it matter now? She's dead. She can't run my life."

Brad was sitting on the arm of the sofa, his arms crossed over his broad chest. He too appeared to be thinking some pretty heavy thoughts, at the same time taking it all in.

Diana strode in as if she meant business. "Neil, you can finish the coffee yourself. Andy, what exactly is it you all think you know that I don't? And before you deny it, Jed and Brad"—Diana gestured to each of them standing in front of Andy—"I saw what passed between you, and I'm no fool. You all know something, and Andy, you'd better start talking right now." She was pointing her finger at him as if ready to scold him.

Neil walked out of the kitchen and rested his arm on the wall, looking at Jed. "Tell her."

Maybe that was what Andy had been waiting for, as he nodded. "You remember when my mother plotted to take the babies from Laura?"

"Well, of course I do. It was awful, but that's over. Your mother's lawyer destroyed the document that tricked Laura into signing away parental rights. We couldn't prove anything, and poor Jules quit because of it. Was there more? If there was, I have to say, you should have said something, Andy. With me acting as your lawyer, you can't keep things from me. Jed, is there more?" She turned to Jed, and the tiredness that had been there moments ago had given way to a fire blazing in her eyes that he hadn't seen in a very long time.

Brad gestured toward Diana, and Jed didn't miss the exchange between him and Andy. "There was more that happened after. You know Aida was found dead."

Diana said nothing as she crossed her arms over her chest, stretching the thin satin housecoat tight, giving him her stern lawyerly look. "Yes, it was so sad, all of it, but I take it there's something else."

"Aida left me something," Andy said. "It was a taped conversation with Caroline where she threatened Aida about something from her past to get her to convince Laura to leave. If she didn't, Caroline had every intention of finding a way to get Laura put in jail on some trumped-up charge, which could have meant anything from planting evidence to pinning some unspeakable crime on her."

Maybe it was the way his wife's face paled that had Jed wanting to reach for her and pull her into his arms.

When she gazed at him, he could see the outrage looking back at him.

"Okay, wait." She ran her hand over her head and turned to Neil, Brad, and then back to Andy. "This is crazy. Why would you keep this from me?"

"Well, Diana, if you recall, when this all went down, you were about to have Christopher. You were already exhausted. There was nothing you could do—nothing to be done," Andy said.

Diana stepped closer to Andy and jabbed her finger in his chest, which was when Jed stepped in and reached for her, pulling her back. "Okay, enough, Diana."

"No, Jed, it's not, because there was a lot that could have been done. You could've taken it to the sheriff, the feds. You should have told me, Andy. Holding on to evidence of that kind…you could have blown your mother's world apart and ended any chance of her trying to hurt Laura."

"Diana, it's not always that simple, and I believe there was a lot more to it." Neil gestured between them all from where he leaned against the wall. "If I remember correctly, Andy, you kept the evidence to ensure your mother stayed away from you, stayed out of your lives. Dad had a copy, too. He gave it to his lawyer."

"I don't know now if I did the right thing then," Andy said. "There's a lot more to it, Diana—the depravity of my mother and the fact that she was responsible for Aida's death. I held on to it because I was convinced that I had more leverage keeping the evidence, letting Caroline know I had it. Because if I brought it to light and to the authorities, any power I may have had to protect my wife and children would've been gone."

"Mommy, I'm hungry!" Danny said from the hall.

He was rubbing his eyes, dressed in his red racecar pajamas.

"Come on, let me get you some cereal." Diana seemed reluctant and tense still as she patted Danny's back and followed him to the kitchen. She turned to Jed. "We're not done talking about this."

Jed knew Diana had a right to feel a little upset, considering the amount of time and energy she'd put into helping Laura and Andy. Maybe at some point they should have told her, or at least he should have. He waited until she stepped into the kitchen and he could hear her talking with Danny about what kind of cereal he wanted.

"So what do you make of Caroline going to Faye?" he said in a low voice to Andy and his brothers. "Do you think there's something else we need to be worried about, something your mother did or set in motion before she died to hurt Laura or, God forbid, my wife?"

Neil stepped in closer and glanced once over his shoulder, running his hand over his beard. "I'd say it's enough that we should stay another day and do some digging, see what we can find out. Maybe it's time, Andy, for you to have a talk with that private detective you always used, see if he can find out what Caroline was up to."

Jed looked to the table, where Diana was pouring milk on cereal for his son, just as Christopher came running in.

"Daddy!" he cried.

"Good morning, Christopher. You have a good sleep?" He lifted him and kissed his cheek noisily, then said to Andy, "And you need to fill Diana in on all of it. She's right. We weren't being fair."

Chapter 26

Diana was buckling Christopher into the backseat of the SUV when she heard Andy call out behind her.

"Wait up! Do you mind if I ride into town with you?" He jogged up, his hair damp from the shower, dressed in dark jeans and a jean jacket pulled over a red shirt.

"Sure," she said, realizing it sounded a little curt as she walked around and slid behind the wheel. Andy climbed in the passenger side and buckled his seatbelt. He slid around and chatted with the boys as Diana drove down the driveway and pulled onto the highway to town.

"You probably have every right to be mad, you know," Andy said, and she wondered for a second, as she glanced his way, whether she'd heard right. Then again, as she had gotten dressed that morning, pulling on her jeans and a cream-colored blouse, Jed hadn't said once that she was overreacting. In fact, for the first time ever, he'd apologized.

"I'm not sure what this is with you and Jed," she said.

"Then there's Brad and Neil, too, who think you need to keep things from me. This thing here, I was a part of it, Andy. You should have told me."

"I know," he said. "It was just bad timing."

She had to do a double take before looking back at the road. She opened her mouth to say something, but having someone tell her she was right took all the wind out of her, leaving her nowhere to go. What was she to do?

They drove the rest of the way in silence and dropped off Christopher and Danny at their school. Andy followed her inside the classes, remaining in her shadow. Each time she glanced up, he was behaving more like a bodyguard than a friend, which she found somewhat odd.

Now, as they walked out of the school, side by side, back to the SUV, bathed with the warm sunshine of a new day, she couldn't help feeling as if there was something more going on. "So why did you really tag along today?" She stopped when they reached her SUV, Andy placing his hand on the hood. He made a face as he glanced up into the sun. This was the first time she could remember that he wasn't hiding behind a pair of shades.

"Because I wanted to apologize for some things and explain why I didn't tell you in the first place. You should know I reached for the phone to call you and Jed when Aida died, but I stopped myself. You were exhausted, you were about to have Christopher any day, and you had already done so much with what had happened, making sure the dissolution of parental rights was destroyed, speaking with my mother's lawyer and the hospital lawyer. We were sure Doctor Richardson had been involved, too, although we couldn't prove it, and it came down to Laura's word. It was you there handling all of it.

We leaned on you too much, and I also knew Jed had been hovering a lot. He was worried this was too much for you, and if the positions were reversed, Diana, I wouldn't want someone adding any stress to my wife before she had our baby. So maybe I'm not sorry about not telling you then, but I should have said something after." This was a reasonable side of Andy she'd never seen. She rather liked it.

"Laura really is good for you. She's softening you," she teased, unable to help matching his smile as he laughed softly.

"She is." Then his expression turned serious. "Which is why now, after hearing what I did this morning, I realized even though my mother's dead, I'm not so certain anymore that the threat against my wife is over. I mean, Caroline had her hand in a lot of things, holding skeletons she'd dug up over many people's heads. She was a cruel woman."

Diana couldn't shake the feeling that Andy wasn't as sure about things as he let on, but then, having Caroline Friessen for a mother, she'd have been plenty wary, too. "One, why don't I let you buy me a cup of coffee, and you tell me everything about the threats your mother made and everything on that tape from Aida? Two, I would really like to know what makes you think your mother killed Aida. I thought she died from an overdose."

Andy's cell phone started ringing, and he pulled it from his back pocket before she could get him to answer. He turned away and gestured to her to give him a minute.

Diana pulled open her door, put her purse inside, and waited for Andy to finish up. She didn't know he had hung up until he opened the passenger door and looked across the seat to her. "That was Brian, the private investigator I've used in the past. I called him before we left Jed's and filled him in."

Diana waited for Andy to finish.

"And he had something, that was why he called?" Sometimes it could be so frustrating with these Friessen men, how they left her hanging as if deciding how much they could say and what they needed to hold on to.

He climbed into the passenger seat. "Come on," he said. "I'll fill you in on the way."

Now she was curious. "Where exactly are we going?"

"To see Brian, because evidently he found out something you and I are going to want to hear."

Chapter 27

For a moment, it seemed that having his brothers with him to deal with some problem was becoming a regular occurrence. Brad was in the backseat, talking on his cell phone to Emily, and it sounded as if there were some issues going down at school for Trevor. Neil was driving, and he too appeared distracted, but then, he also had when Jed had seen him a few weeks ago for Caroline's funeral.

"So when Andy texted, did he say what he found out?" Jed tapped his hand against the door jamb.

Neil shook his head, sliding his thumb over his chin and scratching at his beard. "No, just to meet at his private investigator's office, and he sent the address."

Jed gazed over at him to see a look he hadn't seen before. "You okay? You're looking kind of off. Meant to call you, too, because when Mom and Dad came back to visit, Mom said some things that made me think there was something going on with you."

Neil didn't say anything for the longest time, and then Brad hung up the phone.

"Just have things to figure out, is all." Neil glanced up into the rearview mirror. "Everything okay at home?"

Brad rested his hand on the back of Jed's seat. "Just some problems with the school. One of Trevor's workers is letting him engage in some behavior his consultant has already asked the school to stop. Apparently she's gone to her union rep because she doesn't want to listen to a parent or outside specialist."

"I thought school was going well for Trevor," Jed said. "He's come so far in his therapy. He's talking well, too." He noticed Neil seemed a little more in the loop and a lot more pissed off.

"I told Emily she should just pull him from school," Neil said.

"That's not the answer, Neil. He needs the social contact with the other kids…"

"And you guys need a break from all the stress of school, all the politics. You know, I was reading that a few cities have opened their own schools just for autistic kids."

Why was Neil arguing about this with Brad?

Brad was shaking his head in the backseat. "It kind of takes us backward, Neil. I told you that before. To suddenly have the school segregate Trevor once again…I don't know. Em's getting really worked up. It's becoming more and more that unless I'm there with her, they say one thing to Emily and do the opposite."

Jed really wasn't happy about the hoops Brad and Emily seemed to have to jump through for his autistic nephew. Right now, he was getting an inside look into a system that wasn't too flattering.

Neil pulled up beside Diana's SUV, which was parked in front of a two-story red brick building in downtown North Lakewood. "Here it is, and there's your wife's SUV. They must be inside."

Jed opened his door and climbed out. Brad still appeared distracted. "You know, Brad, no one would fault you if you needed to go home."

Brad didn't say anything as he glanced over to Neil, who was on the curb, looking up at the building. It was clear now how distracted Neil was, as well.

"Up there, come on," he said, paying no attention to Brad and Jed.

Brad rested his hand on Jed's shoulder and shook his head. "Soon enough. Let's make sure Laura and Diana are okay first. This school thing is nothing new, and it's been an ongoing battle as of late."

As the brothers opened the door and climbed the narrow staircase, he could hear voices. Neil was first at the door labeled "Brian Reeves, Private Detective." He opened it and stepped inside a small reception area. The office door was open, and a chair squeaked.

"Hey, in here." Andy popped his head out.

Jed stepped in to see Diana sitting, taking notes and giving him a distracted look. Neil leaned against the back wall, and Brad hovered in the doorway. Andy took the other seat across from a man who appeared to be in his early forties, with mutton chops and reddish hair. He had bright blue eyes and a reddish complexion as if he drank more than the average person.

The man stood up, reached for Jed's hand, and then shook Neil's and Brad's, as well. He was short, with a rounded belly. He pulled up his jeans and then sat back in his chair. "Can see the family resemblance. Was just filling in Diana and Andy, here, on what I found out."

"How bad?" Jed asked.

Diana glanced up at him. "None of this is good.

Andy and Brian filled me in on the details of the tape. I can't believe what happened to poor Aida. She has a daughter who was taken from her and spent all those years in prison because she fell for the wrong man. It's horrible. It's heartbreaking and so wrong. What Caroline planned for Laura if Aida hadn't convinced her to leave…I have to admit, even I was terrified, because Laura could have been lost in prison. I didn't hear the tape, but it's awful, the threat of planting drugs in her suitcase or some other crime she could have been set up for. It's unimaginable. I'm afraid she could have gotten away with it, too."

Diana took in Jed and then settled her gaze on Andy. "I'm also afraid because Brian found out that Caroline wasn't about to just let Andy go his way and live his life with Laura and the kids in Montana."

Neil was instantly alert, and Brad rested his hands on Andy's chair back. "Okay, I'm not liking the sound of this," Neil said. "Is there something we should be worried about?"

"Well, I was just getting to those details when you all walked in," Brian said. "Word on the street is that Laura could have had an accident. Don't know the details. Only thing is the money never changed hands, and whoever was going to be hired to do the job never got paid."

Chapter 28

Diana had never seen Andy go so pale and quiet. Jed swore from behind her, putting his hands on her shoulders. "And my wife, did Caroline have some plan for her?" he said.

Neil was whispering something to Andy.

Brad stepped forward. "Are you saying Caroline hired someone to kill Laura?"

Diana was still trying to make sense of everything she'd heard as Brian leaned back in his chair, holding his arms wide. "Well, just hold on now," he said. "Don't know for sure if it was Caroline, and no one's saying it was, just that there was a job to be done. No one's saying who arranged it, just that something was to happen to Andy's wife, and whatever it was, it was to look like an accident—and no." Brian gestured then to Diana, looking straight at her, all serious now. "No one is saying anything about you or something happening to you, and you can trust me on that."

"Well, that's not really comforting to me. I think maybe we need to take this to the sheriff," Jed said, still resting his hands on Diana's shoulders. Maybe he needed to make sure she stayed where she was.

"I'm with you, Jed, but what about Laura?" Brad said. "How do we know nothing is going to happen to her? This information you have, who did you get it from?"

Diana was watching Andy, who was sitting there, running his hand over his head. Neil was standing behind him, also noticing how upset he was. She ached for him, and she saw the hurt in his expression, as if he were imagining the worst. Losing Laura…it would devastate him. He shut his eyes for a second and gestured for everyone to stop, then pulled out his cell phone and dialed before he stood up.

"Laura, where are you?" He walked out of the office and stood in the foyer, and Diana couldn't make out anything from what he was saying other than how upset he sounded.

"Look, my informant knows everything that's going on out on the streets. I'm not saying there isn't something to worry about…" Brian stopped talking as if he were thinking and then picked up the phone and dialed, leaning on the desk and tapping a pen. "Sergio, Brian here. Remember when you told me about Laura Friessen, how she was supposed to have an accident but no money changed hands?"

Diana was watching Brian and looked up at Jed, who had no intention of moving from where he was. She'd seen this protective side of him before, but she also realized his fear could end up smothering her, so she reached up and covered his hand with hers. The intensity in his gaze was that of a man who was going to make sure his woman was kept safe.

She said, "The only thing I'm worried about in

telling the sheriff is that Brian's contact could suddenly become uncooperative. It may be best if we find a way to meet with him and find out who was going to be hired, then try reaching out to that person."

Brad and Jed were staring at her with such horror that she wondered whether they thought she'd lost her mind. Jed made a rude noise, and Neil strode over as if he realized what she'd just said, then patted Brad's back. Brad was now shaking his head as if her idea wasn't going to happen.

"I hate to say this, but I think Diana's right," Neil said. "I'm worried about Andy. He's got Laura on the phone, and he's got himself so twisted up in knots because he needs to be home now, not here. He needs to make sure she's safe until he can get there."

Brian hung up the phone, and his chair squeaked. "Okay, here's the deal. I can get a meeting both with the man who was to be paid to do the job and with Sergio, my contact, but it's conditional. They want to be compensated." Brian leaned over, looking out to where Andy was pacing outside the office, talking on the phone. He sat up just as Andy walked back in, the tension rolling off him in waves as he stopped beside Neil, looking as if he was about to tear apart anyone who dared get in his way.

"I've got to get home," he said. "I've got the neighbors going over to pick up Laura and the kids and keep them at their place until I get home. I can't believe this." Andy fisted his hand, and Diana had never seen this kind of desperation come over him before. "Of all times to not live close to family… What am I going to do if something happens to her? I can't let anything happen."

"Hey, it's okay." Neil squeezed his shoulder, trying to offer support.

"Andy, I understand," Brad said, "and I'll be the first to get you on the plane and home, but just hold up a second." He put his hand on Andy's other shoulder. "Brian here has something you're going to want to hear. Before you tell him, Brian, I have to say I think Diana is right. We need to set that meeting up. Whatever we need to pay, we will."

"Wait, what's going on? Pay who?" Andy was looking to Brian and then back to Brad.

Diana spoke up from where she sat under her husband's watchful eye. "Brian here is getting us a meeting with his contact and whoever was going to take the job—and I'm coming with you."

Chapter 29

"Seriously, this is beginning to feel like we've stepped into the middle of a B movie. Who the hell does this cloak and dagger stuff anymore?" Jed said from behind the wheel of Diana's SUV. She was parked in the backseat between Andy and Neil, and Brad was in the passenger seat, looking up through the front windshield at the second story of a warehouse, which had manufactured sporting goods in days gone past. The glass on the second level was broken here and there, and it looked like the kind of place where Jed wouldn't want to find himself without backup of any kind, and definitely not at night.

Brian had parked his black cavalier in front of the building and had told them to wait until he'd gone in to see whether the guys had arrived.

"This had better be worth it, and Brian better not be blowing smoke up my ass," Andy said from the backseat.

"It's okay, Andy," Diana said. "You sure you don't want to get on a plane back to Laura? I know you said you have the sheriff there keeping an eye on her, too."

Jed glanced back in the rearview mirror and saw Diana giving Andy's hand a gentle squeeze, but it didn't seem to help ease the stress. He understood all too well exactly how Andy had to be feeling. He didn't know what he'd do if the roles were reversed and he was the one hundreds of miles away, unable to be there to protect his wife himself.

"I know she'll be safe enough for now, but I can't help worrying," Andy said. "Having someone else protect what's mine isn't the same as me doing it. I don't like feeling helpless."

"I hear you, Andy," Neil said, "but I think you're right about staying. Let's find out who this person is and talk to him."

Jed spotted Brian walking toward them, looking one way and then the other. "Here he comes," he said, popping open his door. Brad, Andy, Neil, and Diana also climbed out.

"Are they here?" Jed asked as Brad came around the front of the vehicle, looking around at the parking lot and the empty building. Jed didn't see any other cars.

"Yeah, but there're conditions first," Brian said. "No police."

Jed wasn't sure he wanted to agree to that, but if it would give Andy the peace he needed and end any threat against Laura and his wife, he was game. He glanced back at Andy, who was looking up at the building, ready to confront whoever it was.

"As long as this person guarantees my wife is going to be okay, I'll give them any damn thing they want," Andy said.

Jed reached out his hand to Diana, and she slipped hers into it. "I would prefer if you weren't here," he said, "but since you are, you don't leave my side. You hear?"

He squeezed her hand and expected her to argue, but she didn't.

"Don't worry, Jed," she said, stepping closer as if she understood how thrown he was.

They followed Brian to a locked side door. He knocked on it, and someone inside opened it. It was dim, and Jed held Diana back with him and let Brad, Andy, and Neil go first.

Brian was making introductions, which seemed odd, considering Sergio didn't appear to be the kind of guy who took the time to take names. He was tall, slender, and dark haired, with an odd tattoo on his neck. Jed couldn't take his eyes off the menacing tattoo, unsure what it was. Sergio's dark, cold eyes had Jed pulling Diana closer still. Of course, Sergio's gaze lingered a little too long on her, so Jed stepped in front of her until the man looked up at him, definitely picking up on his meaning: *Back the hell off!*

"So where's this other guy who was going to hurt my wife?" Andy snapped as Brian rested his hands on his belt buckle.

Heels clicked in the background.

"Hello, Andy," someone said, and they turned to see an older gray-haired woman in a tan suit. She looked familiar, but Jed couldn't remember from where.

"Delores, what the hell?" Andy muttered as he stepped forward.

"Who's that?" Diana whispered to Jed. He looked down into her questioning gaze, wondering the same thing.

Neil asked, "Andy, do you know her?"

Andy didn't turn around as he said in a strange voice, "Yeah, um, Delores worked for Caroline, but there was a lot more, too. She was my mother's lover."

Jed wasn't sure he'd heard correctly, and the glance back from Brad said he was just as thrown.

"Excuse me?" Leave it to Neil to add his disbelief.

"I don't understand what's going on," Andy said. "How can you be part of this? You were going to hurt my wife?" He started toward Delores when Brian put his hand up to his chest to stop him.

"There's a lot more you need to hear," Brian said. He was looking to Jed, Neil, and Brad, maybe hoping they could keep a tighter rein on Andy.

"Yes, Andy, there is—but there's also the matter of the money," Delores said, taking another step closer. "As you know, Caroline left me very little. It was always the image she was worried about."

Andy turned to Neil as if to say something, but he couldn't seem to find the words. He looked back at Delores. "How much? How much do you want?"

"Fifty thousand for my time," Sergio said. "The lady, half a million for her favor to you." He stepped into the middle and gestured to Brian as if this were a reasonable request.

"Done," Andy spit out without any hesitation. "I give you my word, and that means something."

Sergio was shaking his head as if that wasn't good enough, but Delores stepped closer and touched his shoulder as if he was a friend of hers. He looked kindly at her, which was such an odd response, considering the coldness about him that Jed couldn't shake.

"It's okay, Sergio," Delores said. "I've known Andy since he was a boy, and I know his word. Besides, I think Andy would want to know that yes, his mother wanted Laura gone. She wanted your wife out of the picture, but that was becoming increasingly difficult. Your mother was so angry at you for marrying that young girl, the maid."

"I don't understand how you were part of this," Andy said, getting louder. Neil put his hand on his shoulder to try to calm him, and Jed wondered for a second, by the way Andy flinched, whether he was about to shake Neil off.

"Delores, what exactly is your role here?" Neil asked.

"I was to make the arrangements to make sure Laura had an accident."

This was sick and twisted, and Jed could feel Diana shaking beside him.

"You planned to have Laura killed and make it look like an accident!" Diana cried out. "How could you?"

Delores turned so calmly, looking over at his wife. Something softened in her expression. "No, I knew Caroline had gone too far and no amount of reasoning was going to work. She wanted your wife gone, and she'd find a way. She had the means, but I'd been looking after Caroline for years. I knew her better than anyone—even better than you, Andy. She'd never have stopped, and the only reason nothing happened before now was because of the children. She waited until you had your baby girl, and then she started planning."

"What exactly are you saying, Delores?" Andy sounded as frustrated as Jed was feeling. Brad, too, from the expression on his face.

"I stopped Caroline." A tear slid down Delores's face, and Jed had a sick feeling about all of this.

"You stopped her how?" Brad asked, gesturing toward her.

Delores raised her chin and looked between Brad, Neil, Jed, and Diana, taking in all of them before settling her gaze back on Andy. It was odd, this outpouring of affection she shone on him like a spotlight.

"The only way I could. I watched you grow up, Andy. I loved you from afar as if you were my son, hiding in the shadows. You're the son of the only woman I'll ever love. Caroline was a difficult woman. I couldn't allow her to do this, to destroy your happiness and hurt that girl. It was too much. She couldn't be reasoned with anymore…so I killed her."

Neil's expression mirrored what Jed was feeling. This entire story was sounding more and more like a work of fiction.

"Caroline died of a heart attack in her room, and you were with her…" Andy trailed off.

Delores was nodding as if he was starting to understand. "Yes, she did. It was made to look like a heart attack."

"But it wasn't," Neil said. Diana gasped beside Jed. Her gaze was filled with disbelief and horror as she looked up at him, sliding her arm around his waist and stepping in closer.

Delores was shaking her head. "I made her a drink, as I do every night, but that night I slipped in a narcotic that stops the heart. I never expected to get away with it, but with your father trying to cover up that it happened when she was alone with me, there was no autopsy, no questions asked. Your mother's body went to the funeral home, and preparations were made. So your wife is safe, Andy. Nothing will happen to her."

Jed wasn't sure whether Delores was expecting Andy to thank her. Hell, he wasn't sure what to think, and he looked over to see the same disbelief on Brad's and Neil's faces. Andy turned around, but he didn't look at them.

He appeared tired, as if he didn't have a clue how to respond.

Delores stepped forward and touched Andy's arms. "It really was a choice, Andy, between your mother and your wife. I made the choice for you," she said. Andy stared at her hand on his arm until she stepped back, fisted her hands, and glanced over to Sergio and Brian. "And the money?"

Jed wasn't sure who made the strangled noise. Maybe it was in his head, but Brad said, "You'll have it."

Delores nodded, then turned and walked back into the dark end of the building she'd come from, and Sergio followed.

Andy turned to Brian. "I'll get you the money. You'll see to it they have it?"

Brian glanced to each of them. "You have my word."

Chapter 30

The sky was thick with dark, heavy clouds that she knew were about to let go of some winter flakes. It was early for snow this year, some said, but to Diana it didn't seem that way. It was early November, a time of year where fall gave way to the cold of winter. It was colder this year than others, but then, it seemed their fall had been filled with a lot of things coming at them, a lot to deal with, bringing the family closer and testing them in ways she'd never imagined. It had been over a month since that day in the warehouse when they'd met with Delores, Caroline Friessen's personal assistant, lover, confidante, and killer.

It was a day she'd never forget, and neither would Jed, as it had been the first time Diana hadn't been sequestered by the Friessen men. They'd discussed, they'd included her, and they'd all agreed to share the payout to Delores and Sergio. Oh, Andy had refused at first, but she'd stood by Jed when he'd said no, they were family—they would share the cost of this secret.

"Hey, it's cold out here. Aren't you coming in?" Jed

said as he slid his hands around her waist, over the wool sweater, flattening them over her stomach. She leaned against him, into him, feeling so safe and secure. He kissed her cheek, and she looked out at the barn and listened to the neighing from the horses calling out a goodnight. It was peaceful, and she breathed it in.

"Was just thinking how much I love this place."

Jed held her and rocked her. "Just got off the phone with Andy."

Diana slid around and looked up at Jed. He seemed to watch her so closely. "And how is he? Laura and the kids?"

Jed's lips quirked in a soft smile. "Good. He's starting to relax a bit, I think."

She nodded. She understood what Andy had been going through, faced with losing his wife, the mother of his children. It had brought about a vulnerability she'd never seen in him before. It had touched her.

"And you?" she asked, because Jed had been just as overprotective, checking on her throughout the day, keeping her a little closer than usual. She'd understood his worry, his fear. She couldn't push.

"With you in my arms? Fantastic." He slid his hands over her cheeks and held her while he leaned in and kissed her so tenderly.

When he pulled away, looking at her in that way that told her without words how much she meant to him, she knew it was time. She pulled her lower lip between her teeth and took a breath. "I'm glad," she said. "I love you, Jed Friessen, and you're going to be a daddy again. I'm pregnant.

Turn the page for a sneak peek of
THE BUSINESS PLAN the next book in THE FRIESSENS
Available in print, audio & eBook.

"A great read that is full of all those wonderful alpha Friessen men and the families they love. The emotions run high and the story is intense."

Aherman

"I have read every book by this author, The Friessens are my favorite. But Neil is the one that always upset me the most. His attitude and the way he treated Candy, but I really loved him in this book. You need to get this book and read it and fall in love with this family & this author as I have."

D. Taylor, Reviewer

"This story of Candy and Neil is one you won't want to put down till the end. I think Neil is the least likable of the brothers and cousins, but he just may be the most interesting!"

Debbie

Neil Friessen has almost everything he's ever wanted:

- His wife, the woman he's always loved…
- His children, whom he never believed he would have…
- And an empty bank account.

Until one day, that is, when he comes up with the business plan.

Chapter 1

"What did you do?" Candy said. She wasn't sure exactly what she was looking at when she took in her husband, Neil. His dark hair had once been short and impeccably groomed but was now curling around his ears and the back, brushing his shoulders. He also had a beard going on, and if truth be told, if someone asked her what she really thought about his new badass transformation, she would have to admit it was beginning to grow on her. She was thankful he had at least kept the beard trimmed, though, and hadn't took it upon himself to grow a pair of chops —because those would have to go.

"Do you like it?" He was dressed in a faded pair of jeans and a black T-shirt that was looking a little worn as he pulled off a pair of shades and tucked them in his shirtfront. A gleaming diamond stud sparkled in the light within his newly pierced left earlobe.

She just stared at her hunk of a husband, who was far too good looking for his own good. He had everything going for him: He was smart, sexy, and confident, with linebacker shoulders, six-pack abs, and full red lips that had tasted every inch of her. He was her lover, her husband, and the only man to ever have stirred her passion.

He raised his eyebrows, and his whiskey-colored eyes were filled with teasing and amusement. They were always filled with such confidence, such mystery, and were so intense that she could get lost in them forever. "It's my new look. Seriously, don't you like it?"

She couldn't help the laugh that bubbled out of her. "One, yes, I do—but, Neil, seriously? You're the most conservative man, or you were, who has ever graced my presence. Where the hell is my husband, and what have you done with him?"

She was holding Michael, who was now walking and into everything, and he even pointed at the tiny jewel in Neil's ear. "Dada," he said, pointing, his other hand on her shoulder, grabbing a fistful of her shirt.

"Yes, Daddy got an earring," Neil said, making a playful face to Michael, who laughed and reached out to him, leaning his little body so Candy had no choice but to pass him over.

Neil lifted his son, who was looking more and more like him every day, up high and then brought him down and kissed his cheek. The man was positively gaga over his children, Michael and Cat, the little deaf girl they had adopted in Mexico. Both adored him, and everything he did was for them.

"So what brought on this need to get an earring?" She had noticed Neil slipping into this change, becoming someone different—not the man she'd married but an evolution, someone trying to become someone else. He was charming, fun, loving, and still possessive, which she doubted would ever change, but she saw the changes in him every day. He listened to her now, and at the same time she couldn't help sensing him slipping, as if he were lost, trying to find his footing and searching for who he was. She frowned, or maybe he'd noticed where her thoughts had gone, as he furrowed his brow and looked deeply at her.

"What?" He made a face at Michael again before pretending to take a bite of him. Michael giggled, a full-bellied laugh that filled Candy with such joy.

"I'm starting to get a little worried about you, Neil."

His expression told her she was being ridiculous. He was trying to shake her off. "I'm the last person you should be worrying about. Seriously, over an earring? I thought you'd like it," he said.

"It's not just the earring, which I have to admit I kind of like. It's this change in you, as if you're transforming into your evil twin." She held her hand out to stop him when she knew he was about to lay into her, probably with some line about how she was misreading everything again and this was him changing to be a better man for her. "Seriously, Neil, I know how hard you've tried for me. You told me you were going to change, and I've watched you over the last year, how you've gone out of your way to put me and the children first. You stopped pushing and demanding and organizing—no, wait! You haven't stopped. You've toned it down some, which I appreciate, but…" She held up her hand again when he opened his mouth to say something. "I have the floor. Let me finish, please." She tapped his arm.

He gestured between them and then wrapped both his arms around Michael, holding him on his hip. "Please, by all means, lay it all out there."

"You sold the resort for me."

"Sale isn't final yet," he added rather matter of factly,

as if she needed reminding.

"Okay, it's in the works is what I meant to say. Your dream…you walked away from it for me."

When he looked at her that way, he gave all of himself. It could be so disconcerting at times, but she knew he was taking all of what she was saying in, as if he were listening with every one of his senses. She was sure that was what had made him such a success in business.

"You've moved us way up here, about as far away from Cancun as we can get, and I'm not complaining. I find it rather nice, being this close to Emily and Brad, and the kids have their cousins close by, even though the cold and damp here is something I'm still trying to get used to. But, Neil, for the last while you've seemed to be floundering, as if you don't have any idea what it is you want to do. That's what's causing me some concern. It's this." She gestured to his earring. "When you walk out the door and say you need to run an errand, I don't know who's going to walk back through it or what idea you've come up with to be your new project here. Last I looked, you have the deck you still need to build, a patio half started, and, oh yeah, then there's the corral, the shed for my horse, and the pasture you keep telling me you're going to fence off so I can have my horse and donkey there instead of having to run over to Brad and Emily's all the time. The thing is, it's all great and every-thing, but you haven't finished one thing here."

Neil frowned and glanced at Michael, taking in his expression, his face, as if studying him, then looked back over to Candy. She wondered for a moment whether she'd hit a nerve. After all, the Friessen men had their pride, and she was pretty sure Neil's had taken a hammering.

"Maybe there are days I wonder, too," he said.

"Trying to figure out what to do...I had my entire life planned out and saw everything happening one way, and then this curveball had me scrambling like I never had before. I get it, it's all on me. I screwed up big time, all because of my need to make things happen a certain way. This other stuff here, I really will finish it. There's just so much, and spending time with these guys..." He made another face at Michael and kissed his chubby cheeks, and Michael giggled and patted at him.

He looked over at Candy with such intensity she had to hold her breath. "But we can't control things, life. It's the other way around. And once you realize you have no control, it's amazing, this feeling of freedom that happens." His eyes simmered with warmth, with love, which had her heart flip flopping.

She was resting her hand on her chest at the open V of her light sweater, skimming over the bare skin, thinking of what this was with him. At times, Neil took her breath away, and at times, like this, he left her speechless. She was about to say something more, but this evolved Neil had Candy scrambling, her mind blanking. At the same time, she was freaking out, wondering what the next transformation for Neil Friessen was going to be.

"Maybe you should call Brad. Maybe this new and improved Neil could use some grounding from his big brother, help you get your head on straight and focused in one direction." She stepped forward and reached for Michael, who went easily into her arms. "Come on, baby. Time for lunch."

When she glanced back at Neil, what she saw was him checking out his image in the hall mirror, taking in his look. On second thought, maybe it would be a better idea if she called Brad herself.

About the Author

"Lorhainne Eckhart is one of my go to authors when I want a guaranteed good book. So many twists and turns, but also so much love and such a strong sense of family."

(Lora W., Reviewer)

New York Times & USA Today bestseller Lorhainne Eckhart writes Raw Relatable Real Romance is best known for her big family romances series, where "Morals and family are running themes. Danger, romance, and a drive to do what is right will see you glued to the page." As one fan calls her, she is the "Queen of the family saga." (aherman) writing "the ups and downs of what goes on within a family but also with some suspense, angst and of course a bit of romance thrown in for good measure." Follow Lorhainne on Bookbub to receive alerts on New Releases and Sales and join her mailing list at LorhainneEckhart.com for her Monday Blog, books news, giveaways and FREE reads. With over 120 books, audiobooks, and multiple series published and available at all retailers now translated into six languages. She is a multiple recipient of the Readers' Favorite Award for Suspense and Romance, and lives in the Pacific Northwest on an island, is the mother of three, her oldest has autism and she is an advocate for never giving up on your dreams.

"Lorhainne Eckhart has this uncanny way of just hitting the spot every time with her books."

(Caroline L., Reviewer)

The O'Connells: *The O'Connells of Livingston, Montana are not your typical family. A riveting collection of stories surrounding the ups and downs of what goes on within a family but also with some suspense, angst and of course a bit of romance thrown in for good measure "I thought I loved the Friessens, but I absolutely adore the O'Connell's. Each and every book has totally different genres of stories but the one thing in common is how she is able to wrap it around the family which is the heart of each story." (C. Logue)*

The Friessens: *An emotional big family*

*romance series, the Friessen family siblings
find their relationships tested, lay their hearts
on the line, and discover lasting love!
"Lorhainne Eckhart is one of my go to
authors when I want a guaranteed good book.
So many twists and turns, but also so much
love and such a strong sense of family."
(Lora W., Reviewer)*

The Parker Sisters: *The Parker Sisters are
a close-knit family, and like any other family
they have their ups and downs. "Eckhart has
crafted another intense family drama…The
character development is outstanding, and the
emotional investment is high…" (Aherman,
Reviewer)*

The McCabe Brothers: *Join the five
McCabe siblings on their journeys to the dark
and dangerous side of love! An intense, exhil-
arating collection of romantic thrillers you
won't want to miss. — "Eckhart has a new
series that is definitely worth the read. The
queen of the family saga started this series
with a spin-off of her wildly successful
Friessen series." From a Readers' Favorite
award—winning author and "queen of the
family saga" (Aherman)*

*Lorhainne loves to hear from her readers! You can connect with
me at:*
www.LorhainneEckhart.com
lorhainneeckhart.le@gmail.com

Also by Lorhainne Eckhart

The Outsider Series
The Forgotten Child (Brad and Emily)
A Baby and a Wedding *(An Outsider Series Short)*
Fallen Hero (Andy, Jed, and Diana)
The Search *(An Outsider Series Short)*
The Awakening (Andy and Laura)
Secrets (Jed and Diana)
Runaway (Andy and Laura)
Overdue *(An Outsider Series Short)*
The Unexpected Storm (Neil and Candy)
The Wedding (Neil and Candy)

The Friessens: A New Beginning
The Deadline (Andy and Laura)
The Price to Love (Neil and Candy)
A Different Kind of Love (Brad and Emily)
A Vow of Love, A Friessen Family Christmas

The Friessens
The Reunion
The Bloodline (Andy & Laura)
The Promise (Diana & Jed)
The Business Plan (Neil & Candy)
The Decision (Brad & Emily)
First Love (Katy)
Family First
Leave the Light On
In the Moment
In the Family

In the Silence
In the Charm
Unexpected Consequences
It Was Always You
The First Time I Saw You
Welcome to My Arms
Welcome to Boston
I'll Always Love You
Ground Rules
A Reason to Breathe
You Are My Everything
Anything For You
The Homecoming
Stay Away From My Daughter
The Bad Boy
A Place of Our Own
The Visitor
All About Devon
Long Past Dawn
How to Heal a Heart
Keep Me in Your Heart

The O'Connells
The Neighbor
The Third Call
The Secret Husband
The Quiet Day
The Commitment
The Missing Father
The Hometown Hero
Justice
The Family Secret
The Fallen O'Connell
The Return of the O'Connells

And The She Was Gone
The Stalker
The O'Connell Family Christmas
The Girl Next Door
Broken Promises
The Gatekeeper

The McCabe Brothers
Don't Stop Me (Vic)
Don't Catch Me (Chase)
Don't Run From Me (Aaron)
Don't Hide From Me (Luc)
Don't Leave Me (Claudia)
Out of Time

A Billy Jo McCabe Mystery
Nothing As it Seems
Hiding in Plain Sight
The Cold Case
The Trap
Above the Law
The Stranger at the Door
The Children
The Last Stand
The Charity

The Street Fighter
Finding Home

The Wilde Brothers
The One (Joe and Margaret)
The Honeymoon, A Wilde Brothers Short
Friendly Fire (Logan and Julia)
Not Quite Married, A Wilde Brothers Short

A Matter of Trust (Ben and Carrie)
The Reckoning, A Wilde Brothers Christmas
Traded (Jake)
Unforgiven (Samuel)
The Holiday Bride

Married in Montana

His Promise
Love's Promise
A Promise of Forever

The Parker Sisters

Thrill of the Chase
The Dating Game
Play Hard to Get
What We Can't Have
Go Your Own Way
A June Wedding

Kate & Walker

One Night
Edge of Night
Last Night

Walk the Right Road Series

The Choice
Lost and Found
Merkaba
Bounty
Blown Away: The Final Chapter

The Saved Series

Saved
Vanished

Captured

Single Titles
He Came Back
Loving Christine

For my German Readers
Die Außenseiter-Reihe
Der Vergessene Junge
Der Gefallene Held

For my French Readers
L'ENFANT OUBLIÉ